Series by Julie Johnstone

Scottish Medieval Romance Books:

Highlander Vows: Entangled Hearts Series
When a Laird Loves a Lady, Book 1
Wicked Highland Wishes, Book 2
Christmas in the Scot's Arms, Book 3
When a Highlander Loses His Heart, Book 4
How a Scot Surrenders to a Lady, Book 5
When a Warrior Woos a Lass, Book 6
When a Scot Gives His Heart, Book 7
When a Highlander Weds a Hellion, Book 8
Highlander Vows: Entangled Hearts Boxset, Books 1-4

Renegade Scots Series
Outlaw King, Book 1
Highland Defender, Book 2

Regency Romance Books:

A Whisper of Scandal Series
Bargaining with a Rake, Book 1
Conspiring with a Rogue, Book 2
Dancing with a Devil, Book 3
After Forever, Book 4
The Dangerous Duke of Dinnisfree, Book 5

A Once Upon A Rogue Series
My Fair Duchess, Book 1
My Seductive Innocent, Book 2
My Enchanting Hoyden, Book 3
My Daring Duchess, Book 4

Lords of Deception Series
What a Rogue Wants, Book 1

Danby Regency Christmas Novellas
The Redemption of a Dissolute Earl, Book 1
Season For Surrender, Book 2
It's in the Duke's Kiss, Book 3

Regency Anthologies
A Summons from the Duke of Danby (Regency Christmas Summons, Book 2)
Thwarting the Duke (When the Duke Comes to Town, Book 2)

Regency Romance Box Sets
A Whisper of Scandal Trilogy (Books 1-3)
Dukes, Duchesses & Dashing Noblemen (A Once Upon a Rogue Regency Novels, Books 1-3)

Paranormal Books:

The Siren Saga
Echoes in the Silence, Book 1

When a Highlander Weds a Hellion

Highlander Vows: Entangled Hearts, Book 8

by
Julie Johnstone

When a Highlander Weds a Hellion
Copyright © 2018 by Julie Johnstone, DBA Darbyshire Publishing
Cover Design by The Midnight Muse
Editing by Double Vision Editorial

All rights reserved. No part of this book may be reproduced in any form by any electronic or mechanical means—except in the case of brief quotations embodied in critical articles or reviews—without written permission.

The characters and events portrayed in this book are fictitious. Any similarity to real persons, living or dead, is purely coincidental and not intended by the author.

The best way to stay in touch is to subscribe to my newsletter. Go to www.juliejohnstoneauthor.com and subscribe in the box at the top of the page that says Newsletter. If you don't hear from me once a month, please check your spam filter and set up your email to allow my messages through to you so you don't miss the opportunity to win great prizes or hear about appearances.

Dedication

For M'Kenna

I see a strength in you that's inspiring! May you always keep it, lean on it, and use it to live the life that you want to lead!

As always, I have to thank a few people. First my assistant Dee, without whom I would miss a hundred deadlines a week. And I need to thank my editor, Danielle Poiesz. She hangs in there with me book after book helping me to hone my craft always. I also need to thank my husband, Inge, who is my own personal perfect hero, and my kids who both are my hearts and know when to avoid my office door!

Author's Note

I have long admitted I'm not much of a plotter. I'm more of a panster who creates a skeleton plot and then allows the characters to lead me where they wish. Well, the hero of this story, Broch MacLeod, was only ever supposed to be a secondary character. I created him three years ago with the sole purpose of making him one of the MacLeod brother's sidekicks, but Broch had other ideas for himself as many of my characters so often do!

It really warms my heart that you readers came to care for Broch as much as I do, and when you guys asked for his story, I was really glad because he'd been whispering to me that he wanted it told.

I love a cocky hero, but what I really love is putting him with a heroine that can go toe-to-toe with him, and that is what I have done here! I do so hope you enjoy the story!

I have taken great pains to make sure the words I used in writing this story were as historically accurate as possible. However, given that I am writing to a modern audience, there are some instances when I chose to use a word that was not in existence in the fourteenth century, as they simply did not have a word at that time to correctly convey the meaning of the sentence.

If you're interested in when my books go on sale, or want to be one of the first to know about my new releases, please follow me on BookBub! You'll get quick book notifications every time there's a new pre-order, book on sale, or new release. You can follow me on BookBub here: www.bookbub.com/authors/julie-johnstone

All the best,
Julie

One

**1359
Scotland**

Why did ye nae tell me that ye're a bastard?
A poke to Broch MacLeod's side woke him from the recurring dream, but Maria Campbell's voice rang in his head as he sat up. He was still clutching his sword, which he'd fallen asleep holding. His fingers grazed his hip to ensure his daggers were still properly sheathed, and then he raised questioning eyebrows at William MacLean.

William, the youngest Scot to ever be appointed to King David's personal guard, gave Broch a teasing smile. "Who is Maria?" He swatted at one of the many pests that had been feasting on the two of them since they'd entered the territory known as the Rough Bounds the night before. The journey from his home to the West Highlands had been rough on the birlinn, and it had taken a sennight instead of the five days they had expected. That put him two days behind the schedule he'd set for himself.

Broch slapped at his own neck, the heavy gold ring he now wore still feeling foreign to him. He'd only become the King of Scot's right hand a sennight earlier, and he supposed that was not long enough to get used to such a cumbersome piece when he had never worn the likes before.

"Did ye hear me?" William persisted, showing his youth

with his inability to discern the obvious. Broch did not want to speak of Maria. Not because he cared greatly for her. They had not known each other long enough for anything more than strong desire to develop, which they'd acted upon fully until she had discovered that he did not know the identity of his father. She had been livid, and it had taken him by surprise. He was always a careful man, so being caught unaware that the unconventional widow would think him lesser because he was a bastard had irritated him and nicked his pride.

He stood, shifting his weight to gain his balance as the birlinn rocked in the water of the Sound of Sleat, and then glanced toward the woods where they would search for Katreine Kinntoch, the woman they had been sent to find. The woods were thick, making sunlight scarce. They needed to get started now and not waste a moment of daylight.

"Ye're nae going to tell me, are ye?" William asked.

Broch spared a momentary glance for the man beside him. No, he was not going to tell William that he'd agreed to become the king's new right hand because his lover's words had ripped off a scab that never seemed to get a chance to heal—the deep wound of not knowing who his father was. It was none of William's concern.

He knew William had petitioned King David to come with Broch on this mission, and he knew why. King David had told him, thinking it amusing.

"William wants to be legendary, like ye," the king had said, finishing the sentence with a chuckle. "The young fool dunnae understand legends are nae born from one accomplished mission but a thousand successful battles and missions. And those are won by a burning, unquenchable desire to prove oneself."

The king had given Broch a knowing, probing look, which had made him uncomfortable. He'd never liked how King David seemed to know things Broch had never told anyone. He did always carry within him a feeling that he needed to continually prove he belonged in the MacLeod clan. Of course he did. There was every chance he was not of MacLeod blood. His mother, Athena—or the woman who might have been his mother—had returned to the MacLeod castle after having disappeared from a summer tournament she'd gone to with her brother, Neil, two years before. When she reappeared, she'd had a newborn bairn—Broch—with her. She'd refused Neil's request to reveal who the father was, or even if the bairn was truly hers. She'd died two nights after returning, and his uncle Neil had raised Broch as his own.

Broch tugged a hand through his hair. He had to show the MacLeods that he was one of them because, in the end, he may not have been. His place in the clan only remained his by earning it every day.

The king had smiled when Broch had finally shifted his stance under David's scrutiny and had said, "This will be a good undertaking for William to build his character upon, and I kinnae think of a better instructor than ye."

"Listen, William," Broch started, focusing on his companion, "we will find this lass, this Katreine Kinntoch, this Hellion of the Highlands, as King David has bidden us. And then we both will be rewarded." Broch would get a large purse of coin, and William would begin to create his legacy. Broch thought momentarily of the king's words:

Travel to Lochaber. Clan Kinntoch and Clan Blackswell are feuding over a piece of land. I recently decreed that the eldest son of the laird of Clan Blackswell, Brodee, was to wed Katreine, the daughter of the laird of Clan Kinntoch, to make peace between the clans. Each clan will receive half the land after the wedding takes place. I further declared that if one of the clans rises against the other, then the clan that breaks the peace will forfeit their half of the land. This should end the feuding, but the bride-to-be has gone missing. If my gut is right, the wily Kinntoch laird is hiding his daughter to avoid the marriage.

"And?" William asked, bringing Broch's concentration fully back to him.

Broch noted the eager look in William's eyes. "We will find her," he said, looking behind him to the rough water that had brought him here from the place he called home. "The king said to start at the Kinntoch castle in Arisaig, so that is where we will head. If we are separated," he added, clasping the too-eager clot-heid by the shoulder, "come back to the birlinn and await me. If I dunnae return within two days' time, presume me dead and return to the Isle of Skye to tell my laird of my demise."

William nodded. "Is there anyone else who would need to be informed besides the MacLeod?" The young fool grinned. "Such as the woman, Maria, ye spoke of in yer dreams?"

Broch's time with Maria was over, and he had no one else beyond his uncle. He supposed he had never pursued a lass to wed because he was always too busy chasing the next mission to prove his place with the MacLeods. It was exhausting, and he suspected that was the underlying reason he had agreed to this particular mission. He wanted time away, hoping—likely futilely—to rid himself of the ever-persistent need that drove him.

With a shake of his head, he released William. "Tell my

uncle Neil, as well." Broch gave William a stern look. "And if ye mention Maria again, ye'll learn firsthand why they call me the Beast of Skye."

William's mouth parted. "Consider her forgotten."

"I already have," Broch said, turning before William saw his smile. He liked the lad, but it would not do for him to think he did not have to heed every order Broch gave him. Failing to listen might result in William's own death. Still, Broch felt a tug of sympathy for William. His elder brother had betrayed their laird, and that was a hard family legacy for any man to try to overcome. The best way to aid William was to show him how to move forward without hesitation. With that in mind, Broch began toward the forest and did not glance back.

Two

"Come down, ye damnable hellion," bellowed Mungo Blackswell. The ill-mannered Highlander stood below the tree Katreine Kinntoch had climbed to escape him and the two other men pursuing her.

"Sheba, hiss," Katreine commanded her dear black cat, who dutifully obeyed, her green eyes glowing golden in the twilight forest.

She had no doubt that Mungo and the two guards with him had been sent by Brodee Blackswell or his father, the laird of the Blackswell clan, to search the forest near her home for her after her father and brothers had lied and told the swine Blackswell and his son that she was still missing. Katreine looked down upon the enormous Highlander and his cronies as they scrambled back several steps and crossed themselves at Sheba's hissing. As Katreine balanced on the tree limb high above them, she bit her lip on the desire to mock the savage warriors for their ridiculous fear of a cat. It served her well in this moment that many in the Rough Bounds were so superstitious.

"She's a devil, just like her cat," Mungo shouted and heaved a rock at Sheba, who scrambled away.

Instinctually, Katreine moved to aid Sheba, and when she did, her right foot slipped off the branch and she lost her grip on the limb above her head. For one moment, she flailed wildly, clinging for life with her left hand and trying to recapture the limb with her other, but her vision was obscured by her hair which slid over her eyes. The sharp bark cut into her palm, making her wince. Finally, she managed to find her footing and a firm holding once again, and as she did, she tilted her head back in an effort to get her hair to swing away from her eyes. The veil of black created by her hair disappeared just in time for her to see Sheba give her a sorrowful farewell look as her cat leaped gracefully from one limb to the next and disappeared into the thick forest.

"Go after that damned cat and kill it," Mungo commanded the smallest warrior there.

Katreine said a quick prayer that Sheba would not linger close and blew the prayer into the wind as she had done for years, ever since her mother had taught her to do so before she'd passed from this life. She added another quick prayer that one of her brothers, her father, or one of their trusted warriors would find her. It had been foolish to venture out from the safety of the stronghold, but she'd been so tired of being confined by the necessity of hiding from the Blackswells to avoid having to wed Brodee Blackswell as King David had ordered.

As the Blackswell warrior scampered off to do what he was bid, Mungo crossed his arms over his chest. "Dark will be coming soon, hellion," he said in an ominous tone that made Katreine shiver. "We—" he waved a hand at the other man that stood with him "—can wait here all night for ye. We dunnae even have to risk our necks to climb up after ye. Ye will eventually fall asleep and then tumble from the limb ye perch on, and one of us will catch ye and take ye to wed Brodee as the king has commanded."

"I'll nae ever wed that murderer, or any other treacherous Blackswell for that matter. I hate ye all. I'd rather be dead than wed to one of ye."

Both men guffawed, and the hairs on the back on Katreine's neck stood on end. Their snickering seemed to underscore what she suspected: even if she climbed down and wedded Brodee Blackswell, her time as his wife would be short-lived.

"Come down and quit fighting the inevitable," Mungo demanded.

"I'll nae be coming down," she called, "so ye may as well make yerselves comfortable." If she was very lucky, she'd be found soon by her family or clan. If luck had indeed forsaken her, as she was beginning to think, she'd have to eventually descend and try to make her escape.

"Have it yer way." Mungo turned to his comrade, the two huddling for a moment, and then Mungo settled under her tree. She could just see him beneath her, his legs stretched out and arms crossed over his chest. The other man remained standing, truly waiting, she realized with dismay, for her to succumb to sleep. She nibbled on her lips with worry. Mungo was right in that she likely would not be able to stay awake, and then they would catch her and drag her to a wedding that would result in her either being shackled to a man she detested for the rest of her life or killed, no doubt by her new husband's hand.

Katreine clenched her jaw. She refused to let that be her fate. She had not been given the nickname the Hellion of the Highlands for no reason. She'd earned it. She was proud of it. Her father and brothers had raised her to be capable, and her mother, God rest her soul, would have reared her exactly the same way had she not died from sickness. Her mother would be railing in her grave if Katreine did not fight to the last breath against being forced into a marriage with Brodee Blackswell, the man they were certain had murdered Katreine's older sister years earlier.

An image of Lenora flashed in Katreine's mind. She'd been beautiful beyond measure and, like a precious flower, needed to be handled with care. She'd been doted upon and pampered, just as Katreine could vaguely remember she once had been, too. In the years since Lenora's death, Katreine had been loved and protected ruthlessly, but she'd also been taught how to defend herself.

She inhaled a renewing breath and scanned the thick forest below her. How the devil was she going to escape? A warm breeze blew over her, carrying with it the faint smell of the sea water in the distance. If she could make it to the water, she knew she could leave these men behind. Not only was she an excellent swimmer but she knew the caves that littered the shoreline of this area better than a man knew the weight of his bollocks. Or at least that's what her three elder brothers always said. She smiled faintly, thinking how they'd been shocked when, at the age of ten summers, just after her mother passed and not long after her sister was murdered, Katreine had led her brothers through the secret trails in the caves that their mother had shown her. None of her brothers had known they existed.

"God's teeth!" someone swore from below, jerking Katreine out of her memory.

"*Yeow!*" Sheba—because it had to be her loyal cat—mewed. As Katreine peered below her into the swiftly advancing darkness, she thought she saw her cat go flying off one of the men's shoulders.

"That damned cat tried to scratch out my eyes!" a deep voice bellowed from below. "I'm gonna kill that cat!" Mungo suddenly scrambled to his feet and raced in the direction that Sheba had gone. No sooner had he disappeared into the bushes than another bellow came from below.

"Satan's hellion!" the man who'd been sitting cried out. He jumped up to turn in circles while attempting to grab at Sheba, who now was on his back. "This thing is biting me!"

Sheba yowled, and the man she was attacking started running, his arms flailing.

"We females must stick together," she said with a grin. She'd hoped Sheba had gone to safety, but Katreine had to admit, she was glad her cat had returned. This was her chance to flee.

Her heart nearly exploded as she made her move. She released her grip on the branch above to quickly crouch low and grasp the branch she perched upon. The swift movement pitched her body forward until she was hanging upside down. Still grasping the tree branch, she slipped her feet up in the air to swing her legs over the limb and swung her body until she could grab the tree trunk.

Sharp bark gouged her already-injured palms, but she clenched her jaw, grabbed at small branches sticking out of the tree trunk, and released her legs. Her lower body swished through the air until her legs smacked into the tree with stinging pain. She bit her lip on a cry, her arm muscles burning as she hung from the branches she'd grasped as she tried to find purchase for her feet. Finally, she felt a branch to stand on, and started to climb down the tree as fast as she could, moving from branch to branch. Her gown caught on bark halfway down, and she had to jerk backward to get the material to release. It ripped across her chest, exposing her skin. Dismay touched her, but she shoved it away. There were far more serious concerns at the moment than her now-immodest state.

She picked her way down the last few limbs, and when

her feet hit the soft grass, she took off in the direction of the water, heart racing. But she didn't get more than five steps from the ancient tree when all three Blackswell men burst from the right and back into the clearing, cornering her.

"Get her," Mungo ordered, taking charge once again.

She didn't wait to see how quickly the other two responded to the command. She sprinted toward a narrow path that led to the sea, ducking a branch hanging in her way, then immediately jumping over a downed log. Footsteps pounded behind her, and fear coursed in her veins like a rushing river.

She shoved branches out of her way as she ran, her slippers poor protection against the rocks she had no time to avoid. Soon, the soles of her feet screamed in protest, her breath came in pants, and the men's voices behind her seemed to be growing closer. Slivers of orange and red rays slanted between the trees from the descending sun, and as she crested a hill, she choked back a relieved sob to see glistening water in the distance.

Walls of rock rose up on both sides of the channel that led to the Sound of Sleat. There were numerous caves in those rocks. She just needed to reach them or the water to have any hope of escape. She turned to see how close the men were as she ran forward. She knew it had been a mistake the moment her foot hit something solid, and she pitched forward to roll down the remainder of the hill. As she tumbled head over foot, the ground pounded her mercilessly. Then it deposited her unceremoniously upon her back on the flat land situated between the rocks. The hit knocked her breath out of her chest, and pinpricks of light danced before her eyes. She blinked and tried to focus to her right, where she knew a cave opened to the waters beyond. Her mind screamed a warning and she tried to move, but her body would not cooperate.

With a grunt she rolled to her side, set a hand to the warm sand, and pushed up, only to be jerked from the ground and off her feet. "Let me go!" she screamed, wildly swinging behind her at whoever was holding her.

The warrior grasped her wrists with his free hand. "Quit yer screeching," he demanded.

Recalling the defense lessons her da and brothers had given her, she reared her head backward into his nose, gagging at the sound of bone crunching, but now was not the time for weakness or mercy. Rage gurgled from the man, but his hold loosened, and she took advantage. She bent her knee and swung her foot backward between his legs, aiming for his man parts. He dropped to the ground like a rock.

An animalistic sound came from him, and consuming fear for how he'd retaliate drove her scrambling blindly across the sand, trying to gain her footing.

"Seize her!" the Scot gasped and half roared at the same time. "Seize the Hellion!"

Someone grasped her ankles, stopping her movement, and then she found herself being flipped onto her back. She started to sit up to fight with her fists, but the smallest Blackswell lunged at her hands and held her down. With her feet and her arms now immobile, her helpless state set ice in her veins.

Mungo loomed over her, his face red, his dark eyes narrowed. He had blond hair that hung on either side of his face and a long, hawklike nose. "I'm going to show ye real slow and painfully what happens to lasses who refuse to obey."

Revulsion swept through her as his hands came to his braies. He intended to use her. How dishonorable, disgusting, and typical of a Blackswell. "I hope I dunnae fall asleep," she said, forcing a laugh through her rapidly growing terror.

In a flash, the giant smacked her across the face so hard that tears blurred her vision and her head jerked to the left. Fury choked her, and she curled her hands into helpless fists, her thoughts racing to find a way to stop this man and coming up empty.

"I like a lass with a sense of humor," a deep voice said.

Katreine frowned, swearing it was not one of her original three captors. She turned her head in time to see Mungo swing his fist at someone, and she blinked. There was indeed another man there now. He was tall and appeared to be carved of stone, deadly looking. She didn't know whether to be relieved or worried. Suddenly, her feet and hands were released, as all the Blackswell men moved at once toward the stranger. He let out a shrill whistle and another man came racing from the woods, his sword out.

The muscled warrior swung his sword in a high arc and brought it swiftly down to fell one of the Blackswell men. The other man, the warrior's companion, charged the Blackswell who had restrained her, while the warrior himself faced Mungo. Katreine scrambled on her knees to the first Blackswell who had been felled, snatched the dagger sheathed at his hip, and stood.

She didn't know these two new men. They could be worse than the Blackswells, and she'd be armed and ready. The towering man was in full battle with Mungo now. Katreine watched long enough to know Mungo was no match for the newcomer, and she could not help but feel glad about that. She turned and ran toward the cave in the distance as steel clashed behind her. The rocky ground made her flight slower than she wished, but finally she reached the caves.

When she entered the damp cavern, it took her a breath to get oriented in the shadows. Once she did, she quickly wound through the tunnel toward the end that opened to the sea, but she came to a shuddering halt at the sight of a small vessel anchored in the water. A flag with the king's crest emblazoned upon it waved in the wind. The king was no friend of hers at this moment. She had to get away.

She darted a look over her shoulder, her breath rushing out when she saw no one coming for her. She fumbled around trying to kick off her slippers, and when she finally managed it, she pulled her gown off with shaking hands while maintaining a death grip on the dagger. She feared her gown would weigh her down too much or become caught in the rocks, and she'd be stuck and drown. As her gown dropped to the cave floor, the warm breeze from the sea instantly flowed over her. With a frown, she glanced down at her indecent state, but there was no help for it. Taking a deep breath, she moved to the edge of the cave and found a clear spot to dive into the water. Then suddenly, heat enveloped her from behind.

"I'd nae do that if I were ye," that same deep voice rumbled, making her shiver.

Her pulse exploded, and she jumped toward the water, only to be yanked back and, once more, against a man's chest. This time, she was not going to end up defenseless. She twisted left and drove the dagger backward toward the stranger's gut, but he caught her wrist easily, stepped away from the ledge, set her on her feet, and twirled her to face him. Strong fingers gripped her shoulder as he relieved her of her dagger.

She gasped and attempted to regain the weapon, but the stranger held the dagger out of her reach. She cocked her head and met her captor's gaze. The bluest eyes she'd ever seen stared down at her. Amusement twinkled in their azure depths, and a smile, warm and inviting, spread across his ruggedly handsome face.

He tilted his head ever so slightly. "That is nae a way to thank the man who just saved ye, Hellion."

She drove her knee upward, intending to unman him as she had Mungo, but he stopped her attempt with an unyielding palm. A dark scowl settled on his face, turning his bright eyes to a stormy blue. "Are ye always this surly?" he demanded, the amusement she'd seen moments before vanishing.

"Only to men who are trying to harm me," she snapped. She gave a tug on her leg and frowned at him when he did not release her. "If ye dunnae mind freeing me," she said in a purposely false, sweet tone. "Or do ye plan to show me what happens to lasses who dunnae obey, as Mungo was attempting?"

A look of disgust swept his face, which both surprised and relieved her. He immediately released her leg, but when she took a step away from him, he moved toward her, closing the distance. She arched her eyebrows, and he gave her an apologetic smile that contradicted his action. Then he furthered her confusion by holding his large, calloused hands up in front of her. "I dunnae mean ye harm."

She snorted, and his lips pressed together in obvious irritation. "Nay?" She set her hands on her hips. "Then why are ye trying to frighten me?"

"Frighten ye?" he sputtered. "I'm simply attempting to ensure ye dunnae run."

"Why do ye care if I run or nae if ye dunnae mean me harm?" she demanded.

"Well, for one thing, lass, 'tis clear these parts are dangerous, and ye need protection."

"I can protect myself," she growled, incensed that this stranger had come upon her when she'd been nearly helpless. She did not like being seen as incapable.

"Oh aye?" Sarcasm dripped from his words. "I could see when the scoundrel had ye on yer back with yer legs and arms held down that ye did nae need aid."

Her face heated instantly, and she glared at the man. "I was making a plan of attack," she muttered, which was not entirely a lie. If she could have determined how to attack Mungo and his minions, she would have done so.

"Also," he said, giving her a look that said he didn't believe her, "I was sent here to find ye."

Her eyes went wide at that, and she took a good look at the stranger once again, her brow knitting together. By the king's flag she'd seen flying, she had little doubt it was King David himself who had sent this man. "Who sent ye?" she asked firmly. "Ye are nae one of my father's warriors."

"Ye ken all yer father's warriors, do ye?" His tone was almost mocking.

"Of course I do," she shot back. "They guard me, so the least I can do is ken each of them." Satisfaction filled her when surprise flickered across his face. She did so love to put a cocksure man in his place. "Now," she said, feeling slightly smug, "we have established ye are nae a Kinntoch as I am, and I doubt ye are a Blackswell."

"A Blackswell?" He looked swiftly to his right toward where he and his man had fought the Blackswells. When he faced her once more, a troubled look was upon his face, but it vanished as if he had shaken off any concern that had touched him.

"Why could I nae be a Blackswell? Because I'm too

charming?" the Scot asked with a breathtaking grin. His eyes twinkled devilishly when he smiled, and two dimples appeared, which made the otherwise imposing man look momentarily undaunting.

It was a lie, of course. His hands told her he was a warrior, and the way he'd wielded his sword with ease and felled the Blackswells revealed he'd killed before and it did not give him pause to do so again. "Nay," she said, barely resisting the urge to return his grin with one of her own. His smile was contagious. "Because ye would nae have killed the Blackswells if ye were one of them."

"Ye dunnae think there are any Blackswell warriors who would disapprove of what those men were doing?"

"Nay," she said, matter-of-fact. "All Blackswells are dishonorable, despicable men."

"Ye've met all the Blackswell men, then?" he challenged.

"Nay." She did not like that he seemed to be defending the Blackswells. "Who are ye?" She was suddenly fearful that this man was an ally of the Blackswells. Perhaps he'd not known when he had aided her that he was fighting Blackswell warriors. They had not been wearing plaids, after all.

"I'm Broch MacLeod," he said.

The MacLeod were one of the most powerful clans in the Highlands, and it was well known that the laird, Iain, was a close friend of King David's. Her breath caught on the thought, which seemed to confirm her fear that this man had been sent by the king himself. She tried to discreetly move away from Broch. "Who sent ye to find me?" she asked in an attempt to distract him with talking.

His uneasy shifting set dread in her heart, and she took another very tiny step away from him. He eyed her, as if he noted her movement, but he did not step toward her as he'd done before. Instead, he let out a long sigh. "I'm King David's right hand."

She glanced swiftly to his ring finger. He wore a large, gleaming gold ring that bore the king's crest. "Nay!" she blurted, knowing full well what that meant. The king only would have bothered to send this man for her if he'd heard word that she'd disappeared. She could fairly feel the waters calling to her to try to escape. She stole a glance to her left. The edge was close enough that she could turn, dive, and flee this man.

"Hear me out," he said, his tone exasperated.

"Did King David send ye here to force me to wed Laird Blackswell's son?"

"Well, aye," he admitted, and fear exploded within her. "Listen to me, lass—"

But she never heard what he said. She twisted and dove, cutting the warm water like a blade, and then began to swim as if her life depended on it. Because, devil take it, it did.

Three

"God's teeth," Broch swore as the far-too-lovely lass disappeared beneath the surface of the sea. He had no time to do anything but sheathe his sword and plunge in after her. Luckily, he only had on his braies, as he'd taken off his plaid earlier that morning when the heat aboard the ship's deck had drenched him in sweat.

He passed under the surface and cut his hands through the water while kicking his legs. He could see her ahead, but just barely. Night was upon them, and he only had the light of the moon to guide him and keep a watch upon her. For a wee lass, she was quickly gaining a surprising distance from him. And just where the devil was she going?

No sooner had he asked himself the question than he had gotten his answer. She angled left toward a string of caves he could just make out.

No doubt, the little hellion knew the caves well. He could not let her reach them before he overcame her. He quickened his pace but did not close the space between them until they were nearly at the rocks. Fear of her being thrown by the waves and crashing into a rock lodged within him.

"Halt!" he yelled. She cast a glance over her shoulder, utter dismay etched on her face. She turned, and swam straight for the rocks, and when a wave came and swallowed her up, he did the only thing he could: he dove under the wave after her.

The water seemed to grip him in an iron-clad hold, and he tumbled around like a feather in the wind. His shoulder hit a rock, and the unforgiving stone cut mercilessly into his skin. Then he was yanked back from the rock, tossed head over foot, and slammed into it once more. This time his head hit, and spots peppered the blackness before him. A small hand suddenly gripped his and tugged him, as if to guide him.

He knew at once it had to be the lass, so he followed immediately. Soon, she had him at the surface, and together, they scaled the rock wall, water spraying them and waves roaring in their ears. When she scrambled into the cave without a word, he went as well. He got four steps into the cavern before she stopped, and he collided with her backside. She gave an *oof* and teetered. Afraid she would fall, he snaked his hand around her waist, his forearm brushing against the underside of her heavy, lush breasts. Instantly, he hardened, and she gasped, wiggling to get out of his hold.

"Release me," she demanded, and he did so at once.

She turned, and though he couldn't see her, he was a man accustomed to darkness, having fought in enough battles in pitch black that he'd learned quite well how to maneuver without sight and to rely only on his ears, the grounding of her heel in the stone and her breath, which had become louder and now hit him in warm puffs, made her movement clear.

"Either ye are a fool or ye're unaccountably reckless," she said, her tone a mixture of scolding mother and worried friend.

He found himself grinning like a loony bird as he pondered how to answer. He was most definitely not reckless nor was he a fool. Diving into the water after her had been a deliberate choice. "I'm determined," he said. The sound of material ripping caressed his ears.

"Where are ye injured?"

"How do ye ken I'm injured?" he asked, fascinated.

"Because ye were thrown into that rock. Repeatedly, I'm certain."

"How do ye—"

"Because," she interrupted, her impatience obvious, "my brothers taught me how to gain this cave by forcing me to try constantly until I was successful. I was thrown against those rocks more times than I'd like to recall before I learned to swim sharply left. Now, where are ye injured?"

"My head and my shoulder." He was not used to having someone looking out for him. It felt... Well, it felt—

Suddenly, she poked a finger in the laceration. "Damnation!" he swore.

"Ye've a filthy mouth," she chided.

"Ye shoved yer finger into my cut," he growled.

"I had to ken how deep it was so I could ken the chances of ye dying from yer injuries," she snipped before wrapping what he assumed was a strip of material from her underclothing around his head. She knotted it and then gave a satisfied grunt. "Are ye injured anywhere else?"

"I've a cut on my right shoulder," he said, grabbing her slender hand as he felt and heard it move in front of him. "Dunnae poke me in my wound again."

The sound of more material ripping echoed in the cave. "How bad is it?"

"I'll nae die from it, lass. It's verra kind of ye to be so concerned for me," he said, trying to start things over on friendlier terms. He didn't care for having to force the lass to a wedding she didn't want, but his order from the king was his order, and that was that.

She snorted. "Dunnae try to gain favor with me. I've nae forgotten ye are trying to force me to wed a man I dunnae wish to."

"I'm sorry, lass," he said, meaning it. "I'm simply doing what the king has bade me to do."

"If the king bade ye to throw yer body off a cliff to yer death, would ye?"

"Of course nae," he growled. She'd basically called him a mindless dog. "Shall we make our way back to where I left my man?"

"If we try to do that, we risk being killed," she replied. "Wolf packs come out in this area at night, and if we try to swim, the sea will pull us under. The tide is verra strong. It's relentless, really. I've kenned many a strong swimmer who died trying and failing to make land. Our time to travel has passed until the first light breaks the sky. Is the man ye left there sharp-witted enough to get in the vessel until ye return?"

"Aye," Broch replied. "He's canny enough."

"Verra well." She moved away from him, and he felt the loss of her heat immediately, but her scent lingered. She smelled pure, like the fresh sea air, but citrusy notes underlay the salty ones. It was enticing. He inhaled deeply, trying to place the flower, and grinned. "Sweet gale," he exclaimed.

"What did ye say?" Her voice sounded farther away than he'd imagined in his head she'd gone.

"Sweet gale," he repeated, striding in the direction of the noise she made as she walked.

"What of it?"

By the loudness of her voice, he knew she was facing

him once more. He came to a stop in front of her, the faint sound of her inhalation and exhalation coming to him. The cave was so black he could not see her, but in the brief time he had been able to, her image must have been singed in his memory because a clear picture of her entered his mind now. Long, thick, golden hair tumbled over delicate shoulders, and dark lashes framed astute eyes the color of a storm cloud. She had rosy, full lips that she often pressed together in disdain. Her high cheekbones carried a bloom of health, and she had curves to make a man ache to touch her. He curled his hands into fists. Lusting after this lass could lead nowhere good. His task was to ensure she wed Blackswell's heir, not bed her.

"I dunnae have time to wait for yer answer," she growled.

Reflexively, he reached out and grasped her wrist as he heard her turn to walk away. "Ye smell verra nice, like sweet gale."

"Oh." Her surprise was evident in her voice.

"Where are ye trying to go?" he asked, since wooing her with honeyed words was absolutely not an option.

"To gather some wood to build a fire in the cave," she supplied, her tone straightforward. "If wolves should approach the cave, I prefer to have a fire burning to keep them away. Ye could only kill so many with yer sword, and I'd rather nae find out just how many before they fell us."

"Verra sensible," he agreed. "Lead the way."

"Keep pace," she instructed.

He laughed, but when she strode through the cave, he had to quicken his step or risk being left behind. Soon, they exited the cave to the rocky beach. The moon was high and bright in the sky, making her visible in front of him. She picked her way across the beach to the woods that lay beyond. He swallowed as hot desire took hold.

She was wearing naught but her underclothing, and wet as her léine was, it clung to her perfectly formed backside in ways that made him think things he ought not to, nor had the right to. She moved with the grace of a doe who'd traversed the wild freely all her life. Her reflexes were sharp as she jumped logs and ducked low-hanging branches. He'd known plenty of women as friends and lovers—a handful who had been quite able-bodied and self-sufficient—but only a single lass had been as one with the woods and seemingly fearless as a warrior like Katreine appeared to be. He thought briefly of Bridgette MacLean as he followed Katreine. Bridgette had come to be brave and skillful as a warrior because her brother allowed her to grow into such a unique, admirable lass. Katreine's family must have given her the same remarkable freedom.

When Katreine paused near a tree, she bent down and gathered all the things he himself would have used to create a fire. He smiled and moved to stand beside her. She glanced at him, her teeth glistening white in the moonlight as she grinned, and something in his chest caught.

God's teeth! Why must she be so bonny?

"Did yer da teach ye to make yer way in the woods?" he asked, needing to concentrate on something other than how fetching she looked standing so innocently in her léine.

"Aye. My da and my brothers. I've three of them."

"It's unusual for a lass to be shown ways usually reserved for teaching only to lads," he said, delicately prodding for information. He'd found that people often offered more about themselves if they felt it was not being demanded of them. "And yer mum must be wise," he added, collecting several logs for the fire they'd build, "to ken the importance of teaching ye ways ye can protect yerself."

Katreine's eyes widened as she looked at him. "My mother is dead, but she agreed wholeheartedly with my da and my brothers that I needed to ken how to fend for myself."

"I'm sorry for yer loss," he said gently. He thought of his own mother, or the woman he believed was his mother. "Has yer mum been gone long?"

"Aye." The sadness in her tone made his chest tighten a bit more. "Since I was a lass of ten summers."

She set down the wood she'd been holding and grabbed Broch's forearm. Her delicate fingers upon his skin were like kindle to the desire he was trying to ignore. He looked at his arm in her clutch. He should pull away, but he knew as soon as the thought crossed his mind that he wouldn't. She had a desperate look on her face, and he had no wish to worsen what vexed her. If she needed him to listen, it was the least he could do considering he was the one forcing her to abide the king's command to wed Brodee Blackswell.

"Ye must listen to me." The anxiety on her face spilled into her words.

"I'm listening, lass," he replied.

"Ye kinnae force me to wed Brodee." Her fingers tightened on his arm.

"I kinnae disobey the king's orders." He regretted that he could not tell her otherwise.

Her beautiful face fell. "Do ye have a sister?"

He frowned. "Nay. Why?"

"Imagine I'm yer sister."

"I'd rather nae," he said dryly, his gaze drawn against his will to the lush curve of her breasts. He pulled it up as quickly as it had drifted, glad she had not seemed to notice. She appeared to be thinking of whatever it was she wanted to say to him.

"Indulge me," she said in a tone that sounded more like one a commander would use on his men than a woman would employ to persuade a man to do something. He liked the fact that she was not attempting to bend him to her will with seduction, but rather being frank.

"As ye wish," he acquiesced, though he certainly did not want to imagine the beguiling creature before him as a sister.

"Would ye force yer sister to wed a murderer?" she asked.

His eyebrows arched high. "Are ye saying Brodee Blackswell is a murderer?"

"Aye," Katreine said and released her hold on him. "Ye said my mum was wise, aye? Well, she gained her wisdom from terrible tragedy." The lass bit down on her lip and looked beyond him, as if into the past. "I had a sister, Lenora. She was six summers older than me." A slight smile pulled at her lips. "Lenora was called the Highland Beauty," she continued, a blush staining her cheeks. Her gaze met his directly now. "Of course, ye ken I'm known as the Hellion of the Highlands."

"Aye," he said, thinking how being called a hellion was much more intriguing than being called a beauty, though Katreine was the loveliest lass he'd ever seen and could easily have been referred to as such.

"Well," she continued, "Lenora was beautiful. She was fair with moon-kissed hair and the prettiest eyes the color of a gleaming sword."

That description could have fit Katreine, but the way she was speaking made him think she did not see herself that way. It seemed clear to him that Katreine had favored her older sister.

"My mum and da had many offers to wed her by the time she was sixteen summers, and they chose to accept an offer from Brodee Blackswell because the Blackswell clan is so verra powerful. Both my parents thought it wise to make their clan our ally."

"That dunnae sound unreasonable." Many marriages occurred in order to join clans.

Katreine paused to scowl at him. Obviously, the lass did not agree. Clearing her throat, she said, "It was widely known that my parents intended to bestow upon whomever Lenora wed half the land of Derthshire."

Broch arched his eyebrows, surprised. "That be the land yer da and the Blackswell laird are quarreling over now, aye?"

"Aye." Anger skittered across her face. "Once the contracts were set, the Blackswells claimed half the land before the wedding, and my da allowed it, thinking they were men of honor. The marriage was to take place a week after that. Lenora—Did I mention that she was eager to wed Brodee at first?"

"Nay, ye did nae."

Katreine nodded. "Well, she had been, but then a young Blackswell lass died and it was whispered that Brodee Blackswell was accountable. The gossip was that she'd threatened to tell Lenora of Brodee's relationship with her and that he'd beaten the lass to death."

Broch had an intense dislike for men who were cruel to women. "Has this ever been proven?" He was not one to condemn a man on rumor alone.

Katreine frowned. "Nay, but I believe Brodee is clever and hides his offenses well. And I think his father aided him in hiding the truth of what had occurred. Anyway, my sister was naive and trusting; she and I had been shielded from a great deal of the world as children."

"But that changed when yer sister died?" he asked.

"Aye." A dark look settled on her face. "My parents heard the gossip and told Lenora they were considering breaking the marriage contract. They were quite obviously leaning toward doing so. My father hesitated, though, because he kenned it would start a bitter feud and there was nae any proof that Brodee had done these deeds."

"Yer father sounds like a logical man."

"He is," she agreed with a nod. "Lenora was certain that if she could get Brodee alone and ask him of it she would ken if he was being truthful. So she arranged a secret meeting with him and did nae tell a soul but my brother, Donell, her twin. He kept the secret, as they always kept each other's confidences, and she went to meet Brodee. She never returned." Hard resentment glittered in her eyes for a moment, and then a sorrowful frown turned the corner of her lips down. "Lenora was found dead upon the sharp cliffs of the Blackswell grounds surrounding the castle. The Blackswells said she must have jumped, but she would have nae ever done such a thing. When my parents recovered her body, the emerald ring they had given her was gone."

"And yer family thinks Brodee Blackswell pushed her from the cliffs and took her ring?"

"Aye. He claims it was nae him. But Donell and Brodee had been good friends before this occurred, and Donell was the one who delivered the message of the secret meeting to Brodee. Brodee swore to Donell he did nae go to meet her."

Broch knew she was not going to want to hear what he had to say, but it had to be spoken. "Ye kinnae call a man guilty on suspicion alone," he said gently. He understood her family's anger and pain, but without proof, it was simply an accusation, likely driven by grief and the need to place blame for their loss.

"That's what the king said, too, both then and nae a month ago when he was here giving his decree that I marry Brodee," she muttered, a frown creasing between her brow.

"Wait," said Broch, something occurring to him about the story. "I thought when ye wed Brodee the Blackswells are supposed to get half of Derthshire, but ye said they received half of the land when yer sister was to wed him."

"Aye, they did, but the king took it back after Lenora was found dead and my da lodged a protest. Da says returning half the land was the king's way of trying to appease him. He was livid that the king would nae hang Brodee for murdering Lenora, nor even demand the Blackswell laird allow my da to question Brodee and other members of their clan."

"So yer families have been quarreling ever since?"

"Aye. My da dunnae want to wed me to Brodee. He fears I'll end up dead, if nae before the marriage, then shortly after. When the king returned the land to my da those years ago, he ruled that if one of our clans rises against the other, the clan that starts the battle will lose the land forever. For years now, Derthshire has been raided again and again, and my family firmly believes it's being done by the Blackswells. They've tried to incite us to rise against them so we forfeit the land, and now that they tire of trying, they are forcing the marriage instead. Laird Blackswell is the one who first suggested it to the king."

"Do ye have proof that they are raiding yer land?"

"Nay," she snapped. "We dunnae have proof. My father's men captured two different raiders over the years, but both men swore to their deaths that they were nae Blackswells. There was just another raid last week, and though we did nae catch the scoundrels, one of our guards struggled with one man before he got away. He vows he kens him as a Blackswell warrior."

Broch thought to tell her that without proof, the marriage had to proceed as the king willed, but considering how he had personally witnessed some of the Blackswell guards treating her, he could not discount what she said. Perhaps those men thought that behavior permissive because their laird did. Considering that and looking into her pleading, desperate eyes he found himself saying, "I will make my way to the Blackswell stronghold after I take ye to yer home, and I will question the laird and his men. Then I will write to the king with my findings if I believe the Blackswells guilty of raiding yer land, but—"

"Ye will find it is exactly as I say," she interrupted, "if ye keep yer wits about ye." She gave him a pointed look. "Ye must be thorough in yer inquires and determined in yer scrutiny."

He didn't know whether to be amused or offended by the way she was lecturing him, but amusement prevailed. However, he swallowed his laughter, sure she would take offense to it.

She poked him in the chest. "Dunnae allow yerself to be fooled by the Blackswells. They can be verra persuasive and appear verra friendly."

He caught her finger and held it. The innocent touch sent a jolt of desire through him. He released her and said, "I'm nae a man to easily be deceived, lass."

"Nor am I a lass to be effortlessly fooled," she shot back.

"I dunnae doubt it," he assured her, feeling a great liking for her that he knew he needed to manage. It would be hard to impartially assess the Blackswells if he allowed a fondness for this lass to settle within him. He took a deep breath. "As I said, after my questioning is complete, I'll write to the king, and I vow I'll nae enforce the wedding until, *and unless*, the king orders it."

A mutinous look settled on her face, and he was certain she'd flee if the king did not rule in her favor.

How could he impress upon her that if she fled, she could invite a dire fate for her family? There were no gentle words to say it. "If ye flee, the king will nae have mercy for yer clan. King David can be unforgiving to those who cross him."

Her beautiful face grew tight with obvious fear. "If I wed that man, I tell ye, I will end up dead," she said flatly.

He shifted his stance, uncomfortable. He understood why she felt the way she did, yet he knew this was the only course forward. He took a long breath and considered her and what she might be thinking. If the ruling did not come back in her favor, he'd have some convincing to do.

"Dunnae do anything hasty. It would be foolish to bring unnecessary trouble to yer clan if the king ultimately agrees that the Blackswells have raided yer land."

She pressed her lips into a thin line, but after a moment, she nodded. "I will carefully consider everything."

Relief gripped him that she seemed to have heard his warning. He opened his mouth to suggest that they make their way back to the cave, but before he could, a wolf growled low from his right.

Katreine gasped. "Give me the dagger," she hissed.

He dropped the stack of wood he'd been holding and unsheathed his sword. At the same time, he released the dagger and handed it to her. As she brought it in front or her, she moved around him and pressed her back to his. It was exactly what he would have done. The way she positioned herself gave them eyes in front of and behind them.

It took but a breath before the pack appeared, one by one, lining up in front of him. There were four in all. Their eyes glowed yellow in the night, and their deep snarls swallowed up the silence. "When I say so," he whispered, "run for the cave, aye?"

"Nay," she replied. "I'll nae leave ye to be killed."

"Aye," he said, clenching his teeth and sword hilt in frustration. One of the wolves slowly started to advance.

Katreine's back slid along his. Then her right shoulder brushed his side as she moved to stand beside him and face the wolves.

"Sorry, Scot. That is nae the sort of lass I am."

"Who's the reckless one?" he asked, but she did not get the chance to answer. The wolf that had been advancing sprung forward, and as Broch raised his sword to strike the beast, it yelped and fell from midair, the hilt of Katreine's dagger protruding from its chest."

Broch blinked in amazement as another beast advanced. He swung his sword and reached for the three other daggers he kept sheathed at his waist. "Take these," he managed, thrusting one at her, then plunging his sword into the advancing wolf. The beast howled in rage, and Broch kicked, yanked out his sword, and thrust again, while Katreine threw the dagger he'd just given her to strike yet another wolf. He wasted no time tossing another dagger to her. She caught it, and he lunged to the left to try to fell a beast that was attempting to circle them. He missed the first time, and the wolf leaped past him. Just as the growling wolf snapped at Katreine, Broch hit the animal from behind, felling it.

He lowered his sword, his body trembling at the intensity of the blood rushing through him. Katreine stood facing him, looking down at the dead wolf at her feet. "Are ye shaken, lass?"

She looked up. Her face was as pale as the moon above her. She licked her lips. "Why would I nae be?"

He was awed and intrigued by her. "Have ye battled an animal before?"

She looked down at the wolf once again. In the dark, Broch could not see the blood that was surely soaking the wolf where the dagger had entered it, but the scent of blood, like iron, filled his nose. "I—" she began, her voice raspy and suddenly shaky. "I've killed a wolf before."

He took a step toward her because her words were coming out very quiet, as if she were fading away. "Lass, what is it?"

Without saying a word, she slowly moved her hand toward her right leg and then brought her hand in front of her face. "My hand is wet," she whispered. He understood then. The wolf had gotten her. "I think I've been bitten," she mumbled, and then she promptly crumpled to the ground.

Four

Katreine awoke to the sound of crackling and the sensation of heat. The scent of burning wood filled her nose as she slowly opened her eyes. Broch was squatting in front of her, his broad, muscled back to her. He had one elbow on his powerful left thigh, and with his other hand, he was heating what appeared to be a dagger in the fire.

She moved to sit up, but her leg screamed in protest, and she immediately recalled her wound with a hiss. Broch turned toward her, worry clear on his face in the dancing light of the flames.

"Ye're awake," he said, not sounding happy about it.

That made her frown. "Did ye hope I'd nae wake up?"

"Aye," he said, startling her as he stood, took a step toward her, and kneeled down once more, holding his dagger in his hand. His gaze fell to her leg, and she looked there, as well, her vision going spotty. She inhaled a long breath, and the wave of blackness cleared. Gritting her teeth, she glanced at her leg again and gasped. There was a jagged, bloody bite covering the front of her thigh.

"Lass," Broch said, his tone so surprisingly gentle and soothing that she found herself looking to him.

"Ye have lovely eyes," she blurted as their gazes locked.

Goodness! What had made her say that? She fanned herself, feeling suddenly feverish. "I need to cleanse the wound," she murmured, looking at her leg once more. The silvery spots came back to her vision and she started to tilt to the side, but Broch caught her by the arm and kept her upright. Slowly, the spots receded, and she focused on him once more.

"I've got to seal the wound," he said.

"I dunnae like the sound of that." She started to look at her leg again, but Broch released his hold on her arm and caught her under the chin, which he then cupped.

"I think it best ye look at me."

"Ye may be right." Trickles of sweat now rolled down her back. "I dunnae feel well." She attempted to swallow, but her throat felt too dry for the simple task.

"I dunnae imagine ye do," he said. "But ye were amazing." She could have sworn his voice had dropped low, like a distant rumble of thunder. One of his fingers was trailing back and forth along her jawline. It was utterly improper, and she should most definitely stop him, but it was so comforting, and her thoughts felt odd.

"My mind feels as if it's full of wool," she announced.

"Good. I gave ye a wee bit of mandrake root to aid with the pain."

"Ahhhh," she said, drawing the word out which had drifted from her of its own volition. She vaguely felt her leg throbbing, but Broch's eyes were so very blue and his arms so very well formed... She lost the thought, laughed, and when he smiled at her, she realized how sinful his mouth looked. It was as if he had used it many a time to kiss a lass senseless.

A strong wish to be senseless and unguarded gripped her. Ever since her mother and sister had died, she'd been told to be wary around men, and in this moment, the effort felt too much. She wanted to release herself from the chains that bound her.

"Ye need to let me seal yer leg now," he said.

She shook her head. She did not want pain. She wanted pleasure. From this particular man, too. Never had she wanted a man to kiss her, but this man, this Scot, she wanted him to do just that. "Kiss me."

"Ye want me to kiss ye?" he asked, and his shock—or was it distaste?—was apparent in his tone.

"Forget my words," she muttered and waved a hand at him that seemed to move in slow-motion before her face. "If ye dunnae think me bonny—"

"Good God, it's nae that." His chest expanded with his deep inhalation. "I think ye verra bonny, but ye are to be wed."

"Oh, do cease talking, ye clot-heid!" She reached out, slid her hand around his neck, and tugged him so close that his heat nearly overwhelmed her. His scents swirled around her, and her belly tightened. He smelled like smoke, woods, and warrior. "I'll let ye seal my wound only if ye kiss me."

Had she really just said that?

By the parting of his lips, she knew she had, and she grinned.

"Christ's teeth, ye earned yer name, I can see. From how many men have ye demanded a kiss?"

"Just one." She scowed at him. "Just ye. But with a foolish question like that, I may rescind my offer."

"God save us both," he muttered. He set down the dagger he'd been clutching and cupped her face in his strong hands.

Impatient and sensing she was beginning to question what she was doing, she gave a little tug on his neck, and then his mouth slanted over hers. His tongue slid over the crease of her lips. She parted her mouth for him, and then he was inside, his tongue hot, exploring, and demanding. Her toes curled at his heat, his mead-tainted breath, and the growling sounds coming from him.

Her heart was pounding, and all her thoughts scattered except for one.

More.

She wanted more of his kiss. She twined her fingers in his hair, and his kiss became almost savage, reminding her of a hunt, except this time she was the prey. It didn't frighten her, though. This man excited her. She returned his kiss with all the desire she tasted in him, and then just as suddenly as it had begun, he pulled back and stared at her with an almost-pained expression.

When only the sound of their labored breathing continued between them, she blurted, "Did I do it wrong?"

"Nay." He shook his head and reached out to trace his fingers across her lips. "Ye did it verra, verra right. But ye are to be another man's wife…"

She pushed his hand away, looked down, and tried to focus on the bite on her leg, but her thoughts felt a little slippery, like a fish. What in the world had come over her? It had to be the mandrake root he'd given her. Why else would she have acted so recklessly?

She stole a glance at him from under her lashes and found him staring at her with an uneasy look. Suddenly, she was completely embarrassed. She had forced him to kiss her by saying she'd not allow him to heal her! On top of her swiftly mounting mortification, her leg was throbbing fiercely. She didn't know what to say, so she blurted, "I must be delirious."

Unmistakable relief swept his face, and her humiliation, which she would have sworn a breath ago could not grow worse, felt as if it would kill her if her leg didn't. Why had she demanded a kiss? What must he think of her? She glanced longingly at the dirt beside her, wishing wholeheartedly it would swallow her up so she'd not have to face him. But since that was not going to happen and she refused to turn cowardly, she notched up her chin and met his gaze. "Are ye going to stand there staring at me the rest of the night, or are ye going to tend to my wound?"

Broch clenched his jaw at her brittle tone. Devil take the damnable situation! He'd injured her feelings. He'd hoped he'd hidden his relief that she'd decided she was delirious, but he must have done poorly. What did he say now? He could tell her that he'd only been relieved because he feared he'd not have been able to say no if she wanted another kiss, nor have been able to stop himself again. He could tell her that in just her one kiss, he'd felt desire stronger than anything he'd ever known. He could tell her that he'd gladly and willingly kiss her again if she was not required by the king to wed another. No, he could not tell her any of those things. It would not serve them well. The best thing to do would be to pretend nothing had occurred and to ensure nothing else did.

"I'll warm the dagger," he said and turned to do just that. Maybe when he sealed her wound she would reveal that she was not as brave as he thought. No lass could be as perfect as she seemed. He tested the dagger to ensure it was hot enough, and then he quickly kneeled before her and set a hand on her injured leg.

She flinched, and he caught her gaze. "I'll be fast."

"I hope so," she said, her voice catching.

"Ye kinnae move yer leg. I dunnae want to burn yer

healthy skin."

"I'll nae." The determined look that settled on her face made him smile. Most lasses would be wailing by now. But not this one, God help him.

"If ye need to scream—"

"I'll nae," she interrupted, looking offended that he'd suggest such a thing.

He nodded, and without another word—he'd learned over time that warning a person you were going to seal their wound only made things worse—he set the blade to the bite while holding her leg in place with his other hand. He kept his gaze locked on her while counting to ten in his head.

Her face went white, her lips pressed into a hard, thin line, and she dug her nails into the dirt beside her, but she held her leg perfectly still. "How long?" she hissed.

"Almost there," he said, still counting, "and done."

He looked down, removed the dagger, and assessed his work. He smiled, pleased.

As he glanced up, her eyes fluttered shut and she started to slump sideways. He scrambled toward her and caught her just before her head hit the ground. Rolling her onto her back, he gently laid her head on the ground and looked down at her. He was unsure whether he should shake her awake or let her wake up naturally, but when her eyelids slowly opened, the decision was made for him.

For one moment, she stared at him with obvious confusion, and then a sweet crease appeared between her brows. "Please tell me I did nae scream."

"Dunnae ye care if ye will have a horrid scar?" he asked, surprised.

"What?" Her brows knitted together. "Dunnae be a clot-heid. That scar will mark me as braw."

"Ye're nae like any lass I have ever encountered." He was awed by this creature whose dainty appearance hid a warrior soul.

Her kissable lips pursed. "Is that a compliment?"

The overwhelming desire to claim her mouth again coursed through him. He leashed his yearning with a hard swallow and forced his gaze from her mouth. "It is," he assured her and settled down beside her. "Does yer leg hurt?"

"Nay," she said, but he could see that she was gripping it just under the wound. She was prideful and did not wish to show weakness, and that attracted him to her more than her beauty.

"Ye should try to sleep. The body heals better with rest."

She looked at him askance. "Who told ye that? Yer mother?"

"Nay. I did nae ken my mother. She died when I was a bairn." He didn't bother to tell her that he wasn't even sure if Athena was his mother. It was too complicated to explain.

"I'm sorry," she said, her voice soft of her voice and her expression gentle.

"Ye dunnae need to be sorry. Nae kenning my mother made me the man I am."

"And what sort of man is that?" she asked, yawning. Then she gave a little shiver.

"Are ye cold, lass?"

"Nay."

He arched his eyebrows at her as he pointedly swept his gaze over her gooseflesh. "Yer skin says otherwise."

"Fine," she grumbled, rubbing furiously at her arms. "I'm cold. Are ye satisfied?"

He scooted closer to her, and suspicion sprang into her

gaze. "What are ye doing?" she demanded.

It was a perfectly reasonable question. In truth, it was a good one. He should not be moving toward her; he should be staying well away. Yet he could not stand the thought of her being cold or in pain, both of which he knew she was experiencing right now.

"I'm going to keep ye warm so that ye dunnae lick the dust while under my care. The king would be sorely vexed at me if ye did."

"I'm nae gonna die," she muttered, a derisive look twisting her lips. "Ye fear the king, then, aye?"

"What?" He scowled as he slid his arm around her slender shoulders and hugged her to his side, enjoying the feel of her when he should not. She stiffened, but after a long moment, she let out a little sigh and her body relaxed. He'd been told by many a lass that he put off an amazing amount of heat. "I'm nae afraid of the king," he growled into the top of her head.

"Nay?" Her voice sounded drowsy. "What are ye afraid of, then, Broch MacLeod? What drove ye to agree to come to the Rough Bounds and do the king's bidding?"

"The need to prove myself," he admitted, surprised to hear himself reveal such a thing to this woman who was a virtual stranger to him. But then again, maybe that was why it was easier to divulge secrets. They would soon part ways, and if she had judgment, he'd not have to live with it day after day.

"Prove yerself how?" She gave him a questioning look. He pressed a very gentle hand to her head and guided her toward his chest, and she did not even protest, which made him grin. She was exhausted, and rightly so. "Tell me what ye meant," she said, fairly slumping into him. He wanted to wrap his arms around her and tell her to let sleep overcome her, but he suspected that would make her fight it even harder.

"Well, I must show myself worthy of my place in the MacLeod clan."

She frowned. "Why? Do they nae ken yer worth? Must ye continually show it?"

He gave a resolute nod. "Aye, I must."

"I'm sorry to hear it. That is surely exhausting, and it means we are foes…"

"We are nae adversaries, lass. I wish to aid ye, if I can."

"If ye say so," she murmured.

He held very still, feeling her body becoming heavier against his. After a few minutes, her breathing grew deep and her head lolled forward. Broch adjusted her as carefully as he could so that he was bearing her weight. When she snuggled into him with a contented sigh, a shaft of longing pierced him. He'd spent most of his life working to prove himself, to feel as though he belonged in the MacLeod clan, and in doing do, he'd not had time to think truly of finding a lass he wished to wed, nor of starting a family of his own. But here was a lass who seemed a most tempting prospect—except she was to wed another. Unless the king changed his mind…

Broch dismissed the thought immediately. It was dangerous to allow such a notion in his head, for if it did not come to pass and he succumbed to her charms, he'd find himself in a dangerous coil. There would be nothing more shameful nor perilous to all that Broch had striven to accomplish than directly disobeying King David's orders.

Five

Katreine awoke to alternate sensations of pain and comfort. Confusion filled her mind, and as she slowly opened her eyes and realized she was cuddled against Broch's side as he slept, she bit her lip and carefully started to extract herself from his solid, too-enticing embrace. She lifted her hand from the top of his very chiseled chest and his eyes snapped open.

He turned his head to look at her. "Good morning." His voice held a deep rumble that made her stomach tighten. God, this man had an unusual effect on her.

"Do ye always awake so easily?" Embarrassment for shamelessly entangling herself in his warm embrace all night long singed her cheeks. She scooted away from him, but as she did, sharp pain shot from her wound up her leg and then down it. It felt as if she'd stuck it in a fire. It burned fiercely and throbbed. She bit down hard on her lip to stop herself from crying out.

Before she knew what was happening, Broch was before her, scooping her into his arms. "When I sleep at my home, I'm like the dead, but in battle or when I'm watching over another, I dunnae sleep."

She heard him, but at the moment, she was more concerned with why he had picked her up than his sleeping habits. "What are ye doing?" she gasped as he pressed her to his chest and stood.

"'Tis clear, ye kinnae walk on that leg."

"I can!" she protested.

"Mayhap ye think ye can, but ye would be wrong. Ye could make yer leg worse. I'll be carrying ye when we are on land."

Through the thin material of her léine, she was all too aware of the gentle pressure of his fingertips against her waist. "Ye kinnae carry me," she objected as he approached the cave's exit.

He paused and glanced down at her. Amusement danced in his blue eyes, and a smile turned his lips up. A tingle commenced in her belly, made more intense when his gaze roved over her lazily.

"I promise ye, lass, I'm strong enough to carry ye all the way to yer home, if need be."

She suddenly recalled vividly his muscles under her fingertips when they had kissed. God's teeth! She'd forgotten she had demanded a kiss from him!

"Put me down," she growled, trying to wiggle out of his arms.

"Nay." His tone did not leave even the slightest doubt that he would not do as she'd asked.

"Ye gave me something which made me say and do things I normally would nae," she accused.

He stopped in his stride toward the water and looked at her with parted lips, which he promptly closed. "I gave ye mandrake to ease yer pain," he said slowly. "I told ye that."

She took a sharp breath to argue but her memories were flooding back, and she recalled it was he who had stopped their kiss—the kiss *she* had demanded. Heat warmed her through. "I only insisted upon that kiss because of the mandrake. I dunnae want ye to think—"

"I have forgotten it," he assured her. She stiffened at his words. God's teeth. Her first kiss and, apparently, she was forgettable. How mortifying!

Realizing Broch was heading toward the water, she asked, "Are we going back for yer man?"

"Aye."

"Then ye will release me, aye?" She was desperate to get out of his embrace. She did not like the way her body was responding to this man. She hardly knew him, but apparently she was so drawn to him that she'd insisted upon a kiss! She should be feeling wary, but her stomach fluttered and her insides were in a tight little ball, which felt more like expectation than worry.

He paused at the edge of the water and studied her thoughtfully for a moment. "I'll be keeping my hold on ye. Ye could drown in the tide if ye kinnae properly kick with yer leg."

The tiny thrill that ran through her at the prospect of his arms around her startled her still. She had to find her control that had apparently fled upon meeting Broch. "I'll manage," she began, and when it looked as if he would further argue the point, she rushed to say, "ye can stay close to me. If I appear to need aid, I'll nae argue." To her dismay, he did not look ready to relent. Well, she could be just as determined as the Scot. "Are ye nae tired?" She hoped she sounded concerned and not as distraught as she was beginning to feel. "Ye said ye did nae sleep."

He chuckled. "Ye're a determined thing. Aye, I'm tired, but nae so weary that I kinnae manage ye." With that, he made his way to the rocks they had scampered up the night before, and he set her on her feet. When she took her full weight upon her leg, she had to clench her teeth against the desire to hiss. She could feel Broch's steady gaze upon her.

Forcing a smile, she said, "'Tis fine."

He arched his brows. "Yer white face says otherwise. I'll be holding ye while ye swim," he said, reaching for her, but she managed to scamper just out of his grasp. Her leg was throbbing, but the pain had dulled already somewhat, and she honestly did feel certain she could manage to swim without aid.

"Ye promised to allow me to try," she said, blocking his hand when he attempted to reach for her again.

"I did nae make ye any such vow." He frowned at her.

"Ye did. It was nae stated, but it was there nonetheless," she said, grasping for anything to keep him from touching her again. The wish for him to do so was worrisomely strong.

She thought she saw his mouth quiver with a smile, but he quickly controlled it, and then a wolfish look came to his eyes. "I promise to be verra gentle if I hold ye in the water."

She blinked at the seductive tone and had to swallow the immediate agreement that arose in her throat. "I can manage on my own," she barely choked out.

Heavens! She'd often wondered why Lenora had not been more cautious of Brodee, but now, with this Scot's effect on her, she had to question if Brodee had caused Lenora to feel like this. It would explain why she'd not been more careful. Katreine had never encountered a man who made her feel so odd, but then again, she'd never come across such a virile warrior as Broch MacLeod, nor had she ever been alone with a man as she was with him last night. She hated to think that all it took to make her lose her senses was brawn and time alone. In fact, she refused to believe it. She was a smart woman. She had a gut feeling this man was somehow different from any she had met thus far.

It was that feeling that made her ask, "Why did ye nae sleep last night?"

"Well," he hedged, "I did nae want to sleep in case ye became feverish."

His admission surprised her and made her curious as to what he would have done had she become hot with fever. "And what would ye have done if I had taken a fever?"

"I'd have ventured into the woods to get ye to yer home so yer healer could care for ye."

"Ye would have risked yerself for me?" she asked, astonished.

"Of course." He held out his hand to her, but she shook her head. With a sigh, he said, "I vow I'll release ye when ye are in the water, unless ye show ye have need of me."

She wanted to take his hand. She wanted to believe he was truly selfless and honorable. She recognized that she wanted these things because he drew her like a bee to a flower, but he was the king's man. Yes, he had said he would look into the matter with the Blackswells, and if he found evidence against them, he would write to the king to plead her case, but that was too many ifs. If he found no guilt on the Blackswell's part or if he failed to convince the king, Broch's duty to the king as the right hand would make Broch her enemy. A little voice in her head whispered, *But what if...* What if Broch did change the king's mind?

She shoved the question away. She could not allow such careless thoughts. She'd vowed never to fall prey to a man as her sister had, and this was no way to keep that vow. With that in mind, she turned to her right, where the rock ledge overlooked the sea, and she dove into the water and away from the too-tempting Highlander.

Broch turned from the raised dais in the great hall of Thioram Castle, where he stood with William by his side and watched with concern as Katreine limped out of the room the moment she had finished her accounting to her father of what had transpired. Broch should keep his attention on the laird of the Kinntoch clan, but he found himself unable to draw his gaze from Katreine. Her shoulders were drawn back proudly, and her head held high even as she awkwardly walked toward the door.

He bit back a smile. The determined lass had surprised him by swimming on her own, and quite well, all the way to the shore. Yet watching her move slowly from the room, he could see the toll it had taken. Still, he was awed by the strength she had shown. He hoped she went directly to the castle healer, but she was a stubborn lass, and he suspected that she, like himself, would see that as a sign of weakness to need the aid of another.

As he watched her pause at the door and then open it, he recalled the morning with her. She'd been quiet and had kept her distance in the water from the moment they'd entered it and through finding William, who had told them that Mungo, whom Broch had left injured but alive, had disappeared. Her only reaction then had been to mutter that Broch should have killed Mungo, a view he could not deny her, as the man had intended to use her. She'd barely uttered a word after that, and she'd said nothing upon entering Kinntoch hold beyond telling the warriors that Broch and William were not their enemies—for now. It seemed she'd raised a wall between them, which was best, considering the situation.

In front of him, someone cleared their throat rather loudly, and he turned, his gaze passing over William and back to the dais to find four pairs of wary eyes upon him.

He almost smiled at the thought that he was glad Katreine had so many men to look after her, but then he considered that they could do nothing to prevent her impending marriage without harming their entire clan. He hoped the Blackswells were not dishonorable as Katreine thought, and that Blackswell's son had not murdered Katreine's sister. But he was trying to reserve judgment until actually meeting them and assessing the situation for himself.

Laird Kinntoch was a tall, lithe man, with long, silvery blond hair and silver eyebrows that framed keen blue eyes. Katreine had clearly gotten the color of her eyes from him. That and the man's nose, which was slender like Katreine's, were her only real resemblances to her father as far as Broch could see.

Kinntoch crossed his arms over his chest and leaned back in his chair. "So King David has sent ye to do his bidding, aye?" Derisiveness came through clearly in his tone.

It irked Broch that Kinntoch and Katreine viewed his status as the king's right hand in a way that was akin to how he viewed a dog—obedient and unquestioning. Of course, it probably irritated him so much because he knew well the king would not welcome Broch questioning his ruling. No, King David would much prefer him to act like an obedient pup. Still, Broch would hold hope that the king would listen to whatever information he presented and take it all into account. "I am the king's right hand," Broch finally said, choosing his words with care.

"And I'm his right hand," William piped up. Broch turned and glared the man into silence. He knew William was only trying to let it be known that Broch had someone to guard his back, but instead of showing that, it revealed that William thought there may be something to be concerned about, and Kinntoch's smirk proved Broch was correct. William gave a swift nod, indicating he understood Broch's desire for him to remain silent, but the damage was done.

Kinntoch snorted, as did the man to his right, who was in Kinntoch's exact image, right down to the bushy eyebrows and the probing eyes. Except the man had not gotten silver in his hair yet. He had blond hair the color of Katreine's, and his lips were pulled into a smirk that matched his father's.

The man leaned his palms against the table and stared unwaveringly at Broch, never even passing his gaze over William, whom Broch suspected the man had dismissed. Broch felt William stiffen beside him, and once more, he gave a discreet nod.

"Being the king's right hand," said the younger man, "means ye are here to do what he bade ye and nae anything else. We ken this. We are nae fools. But hear me... If ye attempt to take my sister to the Blackswells—"

"Donell!" The dark-headed man sitting on Donell's left said sharply.

Broch stored the man's name who'd been glaring at him in his memory. Donell didn't even turn his head to acknowledge the man beside him. Instead, he said, "I will kill ye!" His hands curled into fists, and Broch got the sense that the fool may well leap over the table and try to kill him that very moment. And when William foolishly moved as if to reach for his sword, Broch held out his hands, palm up to show he meant peace and to stop the two pups from getting him and each other killed.

Broch cleared his throat in the tense silence. "I appreciate yer protectiveness of yer sister, Donell." As the man's eyes became slits, Broch added, "I even admire it. But I must caution ye against yer desire to kill me. Ye can try, of course, but I've some experience wielding a sword."

"Some!" William exclaimed to which Broch scowled the clot-heid into silence, but another voice piped up.

"Ye're legendary!" said the youngest appearing man on the dais. He grinned, further showing his youth. "When Lannrick, my brother," the boy said, motioning to another man sitting at the dais who had dark hair and who had not spoken yet, "taught me to wield a sword, he told me tales of a MacLeod known as the Beast of Skye. That's ye, aye? Broch MacLeod?"

"That's him!" William blurted before Broch could speak. "He's nae ever been defeated in hand-to-hand combat or in a tournament!"

Broch inhaled a long breath for patience with William. "Aye," he answered, "they do call me the Beast of Skye."

"Legend or nae," Donell snarled, "I'll defeat ye."

"Ye could try," Broch said, "but why nae wait until I've done something to offend ye before ye attempt to kill me? If ye succeed," Broch continued, despite the fact that the man tried to interrupt, "then ye have as good as assured that death will come to yer own home."

"What do ye mean?" Donell demanded, shoving up from his seat to stand and glare down at Broch.

Lannrick stood and shoved Donell back down with a hand to his shoulder. "He *means*, ye hot-headed fool, that if ye kill him, the king and the MacLeods will wage war upon us to avenge his death."

"Aye," Broch said, confirming the statement. "'Tis exactly what I mean."

"I'll take the chance," Donell spat, shoving the man's hand off his shoulder, "that the king dunnae care enough to wage war on us over the life of his newest lackey. And as for the MacLeods, if I recall the whisperings correctly, ye're nae even a true MacLeod."

Broch flinched at Donell's words but did not deny them. To refute it would only give heat to the fire the man was trying to light under Broch's feet. Still, he did feel the burn of shame and the old familiar hurt that he did not truly have a family. He buried his humiliation and wounded pride. Neither would do him any good in calming this man.

"I'm enough of a MacLeod that ye can be assured they would avenge my death," Broch said, knowing it to be correct. "As for the king, ye may well be correct that he dunnae care enough about me to wage war on ye, but he cares a great deal about keeping his friendship and alliance with the laird of the MacLeod clan, Iain, and Iain would demand revenge for my death and expect the king's aid. So I can assure ye, Donell," he said, specifically choosing to use the man's name so the Scot would understand Broch thought him important enough to remember it, "that to kill me would most definitely bring the king's warriors and the MacLeods to yer home."

"Ye're surprisingly forthright and seem to be honest," said Lannrick.

"I can assure ye I'm speaking the truth at this moment."

"Lannrick is my middle son," Kinntoch supplied, finally breaking his silence. His gaze, which probed Broch, danced with distrust. The laird motioned to the youngest man who'd known the nickname Broch had been given. "That's Cadyn, my last born son, and Donell is my firstborn. Well," the man added, looking suddenly contemplative, "his twin sister, Lenora, was first, but she is dead."

Donell glared at Broch as if he personally had been the one to end her life. "Do ye lie when ye have cause?" the man sneered.

"That's nae what I meant," Broch bit out, irritated that Donell was trying to deliberately twist his words, but understanding dawning why the man was so skeptical of him and had an instant dislike for him. As twins, Broch was certain Donell must have felt, and still did, a different connection to Lenora and guilt at not preventing her death.

"Pay no mind to Donell," Lannrick said. "He's always rude to anyone associated with the Blackswells."

If everything Katreine believed truly had occurred between the Blackswells and the Kinntochs, then Broch could see why Donell—all of the men—would be vexed. "I'm nae associated with the Blackswells," he said, meeting Donell's narrowed eyes. "It's true that I was sent by the king to find yer daughter and see her wed, as she just finished telling ye. I gave Katreine my word that I would write to the king *if* I find that they are, indeed, raiding yer land—"

"They are!" Donell shouted, surging to his feet as before, but this time he withdrew his sword as he stood.

The slide of the steel released from Donell's sheath at the same time that William called a warning. Broch sprang into action reflexively as William did too, but Broch had his sword unsheathed first and knocked Donell's from his hand as the man started to bring the sharp, shiny blade forward to point it down at Broch. The weapon went flying to the right, off the dais, and landed with a *clank* on the stone floor of the great hall.

Intense astonishment touched Donell's face, and then he turned a deep shade of red. He reached to his waist where Broch could see he had a dagger sheathed, but Lannrick shoved to his feet, grasped his brother by the wrist and forearm, and twisted his arm behind his back to bring Donell forward onto the dais with a resounding thud. "Release me!" the man roared, spittle flying from his mouth onto the table.

Broch flicked his gaze to Kinntoch, curious why their father had not been the one to stop Donell. One look in the man's hard, blue eyes, which were locked on Donell and filled with pride, told Broch what he needed to know. Donell and Kinntoch were filled with hatred for the Blackswells, and Kinntoch had not stopped his eldest son's misplaced tirade because he approved of his behavior.

Lannrick and Cadyn seemed the only reasonable ones. Broch inhaled a long breath to quell his own temper. Anger would not help this situation. "We'll take our leave now," Broch suggested. "We'll go straight to the Blackswells, and—"

"Dunnae be foolish," Kinntoch said, surprising Broch. "Ye will both dine with us this night and sleep here as our guests, and then tomorrow, ye can make the day-long journey to Moidart." Before Broch could respond, Kinntoch stood and tapped Lannrick on the shoulder. "Release yer brother. He will restrain his temper until a real need to unleash it presents itself."

Lannrick frowned, clearly not pleased, but then he smirked down at Donell. "I'd nae try to kill the Beast again before ye let me work with ye more on yer one-on-one combat."

"Get off me!" Donell growled at his brother, who laughed in response but did as he'd been bade.

Donell jerked to his feet and turned to his father. "Why would ye ask these men to sup with us and sleep in our home? Why?"

"Because, my son," Kinntoch said, his tone placating, "the Blackswells will try to hide their serpent faces and make us seem evil. I would give the Beast a chance to see how our family truly is."

Broch despised being called the Beast, but he clenched his teeth on complaining now that Kinntoch appeared to want to be at least somewhat reasonable, even if that reason was driven only by the Kinntoch's desire to have Broch take his side.

"I dunnae judge any man without evidence," Broch said pointedly. "Nae yer family, nor the Blackswells."

He half expected Kinntoch to say something derisive to him, but the man smiled and spread his palms wide. "Good. My family dunnae have anything to hide."

"Except a daughter," Broch replied.

Kinntoch's nostrils flared, but then he chuckled. "Aye, except a daughter. If ye one day find ye once had two daughters and then ye only have one, and the one ye lost died by the hand of the verra man who wished to claim yer second, I'd hazard my life that ye too would do all in yer power to protect the daughter who was left to ye."

Broch's chest tightened thinking upon Katreine and the love that Kinntoch clearly had for his daughter. He nodded, acknowledging the man's words. "I would, I'm certain. I understand why ye did what ye thought ye must, but I'll tell ye what I told yer daughter: if she dunnae appear for the wedding, the king will give the disputed land to the Blackswells, and his wrath to ye."

"Think ye I care for land above my daughter?" Kinntoch demanded. The laird shook his head, sorrow twisting his features. "To my eternal shame, I placed gain above my eldest daughter, and she forfeited her life. Nae ever again"

"Nae again!" Donell echoed.

"And what of yer clan?" Broch asked gently. "Would ye sacrifice yer entire clan's existence to keep yer daughter from wedding the Blackswell heir?" He could practically hear Kinntoch grinding his teeth and see the internal war on the man's face of having to make a choice between his daughter and his clan.

"I will do what I must," Kinntoch choked out.

The man would not ever willingly send Katreine to wed the Blackswell's son. If it came to pass that she must, it would be up to her to see it through to save her family from the king's anger. "Let us see what I learn of the Blackswells before any hasty decisions are made," Broch suggested.

"Aye." Kinntoch nodded. "I'm certainly amiable to that. Now, come." His tone and face suddenly became pleasant. "Ye must show my sons and me yer legendary fighting skills. Perhaps, ye could even spend a bit of time today teaching the men some moves? Did ye train with the MacLeod?"

"He did!" Cadyn exclaimed, shoving back a lock of red hair that had fallen in his eyes. "But I heard ye went and lived with the Dark Riders of Conan Forest."

"Aye, he did," William agreed, and by the worshipful look the man gave him, Broch realized in that moment that William wanted to go to the Dark Riders. Perhaps he'd planned this eventuality all along. By coming on this journey with Broch, William was halfway to Conan Forest where the Dark Riders lived, and he had the means to get the rest of the way there with the birlinn. Broch stared at the cunning man, contemplating. When had William intended to tell him, if at all? Had he thought to simply take the birlinn and leave Broch to find a way back to the Isle of Skye? Broch arched his eyebrows questioningly, and William's face turned red.

His attention was drawn from William by Kinntoch, Donell, and Lannrick making the sign of the cross as they all stared at Broch, openmouthed. Broch swallowed his laughter. Some men, he knew, considered the Dark Riders evil. They were not evil, but they did hold special powers, which Broch had seen firsthand.

Lannrick was the first to speak. "Did ye do that willingly?"

"Of course he did nae!" Donell spat before Broch could answer. "Who in his right mind would go live with the Dark Riders? They are abominations. They get their strange powers from the devil."

"They are nae abominations," Broch growled, not commenting on their powers, as he had sworn on his life never to reveal what he had learned. He had no doubt, if he did let anything slip, the Dark Riders would somehow discover it and come to collect his life. He thought they were men born of love between fae women and warriors, though he could not say for certain, and in the year that he lived in Conan Forest with the five riders, he had seen things which could not be explained, and hardly believed, but were so. "I went there of my own choosing. I was nae punished and sent there."

"Why in God's name would ye live in Conan Forest?" Donell demanded. "'Tis rumored to be deep in the bowels of the Earth, with ground made of broken rock, rivers that rush so fast ye risk yer life merely stepping into them, and swampy meadows that ye must wade through to even get to the forest." Donell's voice had gone low, as if he were telling a spooky story around a campfire to his brothers. "'Tis said that in the meadow lie snakes and creatures that will pull ye under the muck, which will fill yer lungs and kill ye."

Broch snorted at that, though it was all true. Then he repeated that which he had vowed to say of his time there. "I did nae ever see any creatures in the meadows, but they are most assuredly swampy and full of snakes. And the thick slime does surround the forest, which is unusually made up of rocky ground and precious little mossy green. The river does rush fast and deep, and it's so cold yer bollocks dunnae drop for an entire day after ye've been in the icy water."

Lannrick, Cadyn, and William groaned in unison at that, to which Broch grinned.

"So why did ye go live among the Dark Riders?" Lannrick inquired.

The question stirred memories Broch had long refused to recall. He'd gone when he was a lad of fourteen summers, after an instance of being particularly humiliated for being a bastard. Broch locked gazes with William once more. It had been William's older brother Stein who had given Broch the beating. Stein was not a good man.

William hung his head in shame for an act he had no part of. Broch had already told him not to carry the burden, but he saw now that William carried all the weight for the sins of his family. Stein had taken offense to the lass he liked having a tendre for Broch instead of himself. The older boy had handily defeated Broch in one-on-one combat in the tournament that the MacLeans had been participating in, but that humiliation had not been enough for the man, Stein.

Stein and his friends had gone into Broch's tent that night while he was sleeping, had stripped him naked, dragged him outside, and tied him to a post in the center of the tents of all the clans gathered for the tournament. They painted the word *bastard* on his chest in sheep's blood. They'd left him there until the next morning for all the clans to see.

Broch would never forget the bone-deep, burning humiliation. Iain had been so furious, Broch had feared it would cause a war between the MacLeods and the

MacLeans, who had long been allies. Instead, Alex MacLean, the laird, had cast Stein and all who had helped him out of the MacLean clan, saving the clans from becoming enemies. And Alex, four summers older than Broch, had advised Broch to train harder and become as undefeatable as any man could be, because there would always be fools who used the fact that Broch did not know who his father was as a reason not to respect him. Unless he could demand it.

When Lannrick cleared his throat, Broch realized he'd been standing there lost in his memories and had not answered the man. "I went because I wished to create a name, as I had none that was truly my own. I kenned that if I became a great warrior, I could. I'd heard of the Dark Riders, same as ye. I'd heard they were feared warriors that had never been beaten in battle, and that they had unusual training methods and sometimes took in outsiders if they deemed the outsider worthy."

"How did ye get them to take ye in?" Cadyn asked, awe in his voice. Broch noted the way William stilled and leaned in as if not to miss a word.

He'd revealed to the Dark Riders that he was a bastard, and he wanted respect. They had understood that, though they had told Broch that the only respect he truly needed was respect for himself and a belief in himself. He was not about to share those things, though.

"I think they could see how verra much I wanted to prove myself to others," he said instead, which was the truth without all the details.

"Can ye show us some of the things ye learned in yer time there?" Cadyn asked, to which William nodded.

"I dunnae care to see anything he learned," Donell snapped.

"Ye should, ye clot-heid," Lannrick bit back. "He just knocked yer sword out of yer hand without so much as batting an eyelash."

"We'll all go watch him," Kinntoch announced, giving an unmistakable warning look to his eldest son. "Come," the laird said. He descended the dais and motioned to Broch. "Tell me of the MacLeod as we walk. I kenned his father but not the man who is laird now. Iain?"

"Aye. Iain," Broch confirmed and began to talk of him. But he could not help wondering if Kinntoch was merely curious or if he was intent on discovering just how great of an opponent Iain would be if the Kinntoch did decide to disobey the king's orders and start a war.

Six

Katreine gave a half-hearted glance around the loch adjacent to her family's castle, ensured no one was near, and stripped down to her léine to wade into the water. Everyone knew she swam in the loch at night before supper, so no one should dare to come here. It was her private time. As she glided through the water, she felt the tension of the day, the strain created by inability to get Broch MacLeod out of her head, finally slipping away. She knew from speaking with her father that Broch and William would sup with them tonight, and tomorrow they would make their way to the Blackswell holding. Broch had promised not only her but her father and brothers that he would do his best to discover if the Blackswells were raiding their lands, and if they were, Broch had vowed to inform the king.

Her father had impressed upon her the importance of making Broch like them tonight, as Da implied that the fonder Broch felt toward them, the more inclined he'd be to take their side against the Blackswells and not accept the false face the Blackswells were certain to present to him. The mere idea of being near him again made her stomach flutter.

It vexed her to no end that despite telling herself she'd be guarded around him, she had been unable to put him from her mind. In fact, she'd thought of little else but him all day. When the healer was inspecting her wound this morning, Katreine had recalled the concern he'd shown her and the gentle care he'd given her. When she'd been bathing to wash away the grime from the whole ordeal, she vividly had remembered the heat of his hands upon her and the warmth of his mouth as their tongues intertwined. When she'd been in the kitchens helping to prepare supper, she'd been lost in thoughts of his seductive blue eyes and the way every single thing about the man, from his broad chest, to his powerful thighs, to the rippling muscles of his arms, to the way he wielded a sword, exuded raw masculinity and coiled power just waiting to unleash.

"God's teeth," she moaned, flipping onto her back to gaze upon the moon and stars. She prayed she could conquer her fascination and pull to this man she had just met.

She frowned at the twinkling stars as an image of Broch crept back into her mind. Och! She tried again to focus on something else as she floated under the high cliffs. With her eyes, she followed the line of the sharp, jagged ledge from which she often jumped into the water. For a brief moment, her heart ceased. She could have sworn she saw the silhouette of a man standing on the ridge, but then there was nothing.

She blinked and peered into the dark above. There were parting shadows but not even a glimmer of what she had thought she'd seen. Her mind was playing tricks on her, teasing her with a giant figure that reminded her of Broch. She rubbed her eyes, looked again, and still there was nothing but the rocks. The shadow was gone, just as Broch MacLeod would be on the morrow. Then she could put his probing eyes, hard muscles, and honorable deeds out of her mind. Tonight, she would be pleasant, dignified, distant, and—

A splash immediately to her right sent water over her and rolled her to the right, making her scream. She came up spewing water from her mouth and blinking. Her pulse exploded when she thought of her defenseless state, and as whoever had jumped from the cliff surged to the surface, she used the only weapon she had—her fist. She shot it out and into the chin of the man who dared to invade her private time. Her knuckles connected not with bone, as she had been expecting, but with a grip harder than any she had ever experienced. She hissed, and the iron grasp immediately lessened, and then a low, deep, familiar chuckle rolled around her.

"Lass," Broch said, "why is it that every time we encounter each other, ye try to wound me? Do ye do that to all men?"

"Nay," she said, wincing at her breathless voice, which had nothing to do with the fright he'd caused her and everything to do with his nearness and the way he overwhelmed all her senses. "But ye are the only man I've ever known who dunnae take a care around me."

She gasped. That was it! That was why she was pulled to him. Men who'd thought to woo her had approached her as if she were a fragile thing that might break or as if they were fearful of what her father or brothers would do if they did not treat her like a delicate flower. Except, of course, the Blackswell warriors who had attempted to snatch her. But from the moment she met Broch, he seemed to see her as woman to be taken seriously.

She grinned at him, and he frowned. "Am I to assume by the smile on yer face that ye dunnae mind that I'm wary of ye?" he asked.

"Well, to be honest, I love it," she found herself admitting. "I've worked verra hard to be able to defend myself, and I love that ye recognize how a woman can be deadly, too."

"Trust me," he said with a laugh, "I recognize it. It's a foolish man indeed who dunnae seek to defend himself against a woman who is vexed."

Why did he have to say such things? The sort of things that made her stomach tighten and her guard slip?

She cleared her throat, determined to stay vigilant. "What are ye doing in the loch?" she asked, instilling her normal suspicion in her voice.

"Diving for lasses," he responded immediately and chuckled.

She had to swallow the desire to laugh with him. "Do be serious," she chided, but it was hard to remain serious herself with his hand still firmly closed around hers as they floated face-to-face. She wiggled her fingers and tugged.

"Oh," he said, and she could see well enough in the moonlight to know his eyes had widened and he was now staring at their hands. Had he not realized he still was holding her hand? Did that mean he was as distracted by her as she was him?

Heavens! The foolish side of her was determined to break free.

"I vow that if ye release me," she teased, "I'll nae strike ye."

His laugher was so full-hearted, so natural, that her defenses slipped and she joined in. He released her hand, but neither of them moved. They treaded water there, facing each other, and she laughed as she had never done before with another. It felt wondrous and dangerous. She sensed that same tug to him as she had before, and she struggled against giving in to it.

She started to stroke backward, away from him, when he said, "I like yer brothers Cadyn and Lannrick."

She paused and floated for a moment. Here was an opportunity to bring Broch further to their side and against the Blackswells, and she would be a fool not to use it, so she swam back to him. "Cadyn liked ye and William verra much," she said. "He told me William shoots a bow truer than any man he has ever seen, and he said that ye showed him and Lannrick some excellent fighting techniques today."

"That's kind of him," he said. The way the moon glinted off the rich outlines of his shoulders made muscles tighten at her core, muscles she had not known she possessed. She swallowed and tried to recall where she'd been going with her conversation. It took a moment, but she remembered.

"Where did ye learn to fight so well?" she asked, though she already knew. Broch, it seemed, had won Cadyn's admiration almost immediately. Of course, Cadyn dreamed of becoming a legendary warrior, which Broch apparently already was, and when she had run into Cadyn in the courtyard earlier, he'd wanted to do nothing but speak of Broch, and so had William, who was obviously in awe of Broch as well.

Her father and Donell had come into the courtyard shortly after Cadyn and William had departed to ride, and she'd seen instantly the dislike for Broch in Donell's eyes. And when he'd called Broch *the king's bastard*, she'd had to clench her teeth on snapping at her brother. She had managed to say, in a very pleasant tone, that Donell should not judge a man he'd only just met. It had earned her an often-heard lecture from Donell and her father on the dangers of not being suspicious of men outside of her family or clan.

"Well, the MacLeods taught me much of what I ken," Broch said, pulling her thoughts back to him, "but I also went to train and live with the Dark Riders for a year."

"Was that difficult?" She circled her arms in the water. "To leave yer home?"

"Nae at the time," he said, surprising her.

"Ye were nae happy there?"

"I was mostly, but then I got in a fight with a warrior from the MacLean clan, who was at Dunvegan for the annual summer tourney the MacLeods host. He taunted and humiliated me, and I vowed I'd nae ever be in position to allow a man to do that to me again."

"Dunnae ye mean '*we* MacLeods'?" she said, recalling what he'd said in the cave about needing to prove himself. She wondered why that was. Why did he not feel a part of his own clan?

"Has anyone ever told ye that ye're verra astute?"

"Aye. I've had several hopeful men who wished to woo me remark that I was too shrewd for what a woman should be."

Suddenly, Broch was very near her. She blinked, not knowing if a slight current had pulled them together or if he purposely had swum closer. Either way, she didn't move, even knowing she should. The man had her courting danger! The air between them seemed to crackle as he said, "Those men are fools. There is nothing more beguiling than a clever lass."

How could it be that she floated in cool water, yet she suddenly felt so hot? She grasped her hair and twined it in a coil to get it off her neck and feel the breeze. "Dunnae try to avoid my question," she said, immensely relieved that she had remembered that she'd asked it. "Do ye nae consider yerself a MacLeod?"

"Aye and nay. Most of them have made me feel like one of them, especially my laird and his family. But a sense of nae truly being a MacLeod hangs over me. I dunnae ken who my father was, nor am I certain if the woman I always believed to be my mother actually was. So the need to prove myself is always there, which is why I'm here... I dunnae expect ye to understand."

Impulsively, she pressed a finger to his lips. "But I do," she said, her heart racing. "I ken the caves as well as I do because I worked hard to learn them, to prove to my brothers and my da that they dunnae need to guard me constantly, fash for me always. I had hoped that if I could prove this, they would find a measure of peace, and that the guilt they feel because of my sister's death would lessen." She paused a moment. "I feel as if they are always watching and waiting for me to fall prey to a horrible man as Lenora did. I kinnae fail them or give them more cause for concern."

The minute the sentence was out of her mouth, astonishment hit her. She had not truly realized she felt that way until this moment. God's teeth! She was supposed to be wary and guarded, and instead she was blabbering on, revealing secrets she had not known she was keeping. "I need to return to the keep," she declared. Without waiting for his response, she turned to swim away from him, but his hand clasped her wrist and she found herself being tugged backward and turned to face him.

"What are ye doing?" she gasped, as her eyes locked with his.

"Something dangerous," he replied, his mouth hungrily covering hers.

As Broch claimed Katreine's sweet mouth, and her body pressed hard against his, all reason, all caution, all good sense fled him. He gave himself over to the passion she had stirred in him by simply floating in the loch under the moonlight and being her open, honest self. He felt in the way she was digging her hands into his hair and heard in the whimpers coming from her that the hot tide of desire flowing through him was also raging inside her. And God help him, he was not concerned that he was kissing a woman the king wished to wed to another. Victory, that this lass, who was so guarded, was allowing him to kiss her consumed him.

It was the last coherent thought he had. He slipped his arm around her waist to hold her firmly to him and keep them both afloat, and all he could think of was the need to taste more of her. He broke away from her hot, honeyed mouth to trail fiery kisses over her wet, salty skin. Her mouth came to his neck, and she suckled him, making him groan.

Need pounded through him as he found one of her hard buds with his fingers and then, in desperation, slipped her léine over her breast to suckle that nipple. She gasped but did not pull away, and when his mouth covered her bud, he pulled on it and circled it with his tongue until she cried out and arched against him, her nails raking his back under the water.

Suddenly, male laughter filled the night. Broch froze, then in a rush of movement, brought Katreine's léine back up to cover her as he turned to see who was at the loch. But Katreine pulled him back around and hissed, "My brothers! 'Tis my brothers! Why would they come here? They ken I swim here before supper."

Broch frowned at that. Cadyn was the one who had suggested Broch go to the loch to take a dip. Had he intended for Broch to happen on Katreine?

She hissed between her teeth. "If they find us here like this—"

He did not need her to finish the sentence. "Dive," he commanded, and together, they went under the water. She took his hand and started to guide him. He followed, and when they came up moments later, they were in the cave.

"We can make our way through the woods to the keep," she assured him.

He nodded, his blood still rushing from the desire and the adrenaline to keep her safe. He'd never in his life lost control like that. She could soon be wed to another, and honor would not allow that he impede that. "Katreine, I should nae have done that. I'm sorry."

"I could have stopped ye," she said, her voice low. And though he could not see her in the darkness, he sensed she was looking at him. Then her warm breath tickled his chest, and she pressed a palm to his heart. "I could have stopped ye, but I did nae want to, so dunnae blame just yerself. Mayhap if the king revokes his command that I wed Brodee… Well, mayhap then…"

Her sentence trailed off, but he understood what she meant. Maybe then they could see where this led. He covered her hand with his and brushed a gentle kiss across her lips. "I'd like that verra much," he assured her.

"I'll head to the keep first. Ye wait to follow so we are nae seen returning together."

He nodded, and she departed without a word. He sat, recalling the kiss and then thinking upon his duty to be objective with the Blackswells. Could he still be? He *had* to be. No matter what, he would be thorough and fair.

The last thought brought an unwelcome one. Had Cadyn purposely sent him here hoping something would occur between him and Katreine so that Broch would be more inclined to favor them over the Blackswells? Whether it was purposeful or not, Broch had to depart tonight for Hightower Castle. Another kiss from Katreine like the one they'd just shared and he feared that no matter how much he wanted to be impartial toward the Blackswells, it would be impossible. The best thing to do would be to leave immediately, especially since everything within him rebelled against the notion.

Seven

Broch and William entered Blackswell land a day after leaving Katreine's home. Broch's guilt about not saying farewell to Katreine was in the back of his mind as he maneuvered his horse up the narrow path that wound around the mountain on which the Blackswell keep was perched. Broch glanced up at the towering Blackswell stronghold, impressed by its size and the strategic location of where it had been built.

Three sides of the stronghold were surrounded by the sea. The castle was inaccessible by two of those sides because the water went straight to rock that jutted up high into the sky. But on one side, there was a small section of beach where vessels could be docked, and there appeared to be steps carved into the rock leading up to the main keep.

The architecture reminded him somewhat of Dunvegan Castle in that the MacLeod stronghold also met water on two sides, and on the third side, where the beach for landing vessels was, there were steep seagate stairs, like the Blackswells' castle, Hightower. But the path of stairs here was much narrower than at Dunvegan. On the side of Hightower that was not met by water, there was one singular path wide enough for horses to traverse only in a single line, which he and William had done.

The path widened as they reached the top of the mountain, and at the pinnacle, Hightower rose toward the heavens. The castle had been aptly named as it consisted of a large keep in the middle and four towers that stood tall on all four corners of the castle grounds. The towers were connected by bridges in the air, and Broch now saw that they were manned by ten guards upon the bridges. The towers, alight with torches, appeared to be manned by two guards per tower. If it came to a war between the Kinntochs and the Blackswells, the Blackswell castle would be much harder to breach than Thioram.

The thought brought Katreine swiftly back to his mind. Had she been vexed when she'd learned he'd left without bidding her farewell? He'd told her father, of course, and the smug smile he had given Broch made his suspicion grow that he'd purposely been sent to that loch to encounter Katreine. He refused to consider if Katreine had been a willing participant since he was not even certain there was subterfuge. Besides, he needed to be completely concentrated on the Blackswells.

As Broch and William pulled their horses up to the small guard towers at the gate of the keep, two Blackswell soldiers greeted them with drawn swords. Torches flickered from pikes in the ground, so Broch could see well what the warriors looked like. The men appeared sinewy, their faces hard and their eyes unfriendly. But they were the first line of defense against any who wished for entrance into the Blackswell stronghold, so it made good sense for the Blackswell laird to have two of his harsher warriors at the gate.

"Speak yer business," the warrior with hair the color of night demanded.

"I am King David's right hand, Broch MacLeod." Broch motioned to William. "This is William MacLean, one of the king's personal guards. I'm here by order of the king to see that the wedding of Brodee Blackswell and Katreine Kinntoch occurs." His chest tightened at his words. He gritted his teeth, burying his newfound desire for the lass, and tried to narrow his thoughts to his mission and the vow he had made to Katreine and her family.

"We dunnae need ye to aid us in seeing that the wedding occurs," the man snarled. "We have it in hand."

"Do ye now?" Broch kept his tone calm, though the man was annoying. "If by 'in hand,' ye refer to the men that were sent to collect the Kinntoch lass, then ye'd do well to ken that those men are dead."

Steel swished through the air as the dark-headed guard tried to bring his sword to Broch's chest. But Broch swung his sword up faster and met the man's weapon midair while William handily did the same with the other guard, grinning like a clot-heid who had no fear his life could be ended. Broch truly needed to have a serious talk with William.

"Did ye kill our men?" the guard snarled.

"Aye," Broch replied. "Because they tried to kill me after I witnessed them about to abuse Katreine Kinntoch. I suggest ye make haste to inform yer laird that I am here. He has questions to answer, and if I dunnae like the answers he gives, then I'll be recommending to the king that the wedding nae occur." When the man glared at Broch, he said, "I'm happy to fight ye, but I dunnae think it will please yer laird to discover ye battled the king's man."

The man jerked his head. "Follow me," he growled.

Broch motioned to William to come, as well, and the two of them dropped into step behind the guard while the other Blackswell warrior brought up the back of their progression.

William grinned at Broch. "We handled that well."

Broch scowled at William until the grin slid from the younger man's face. "Ye handled it like a man who dunnae have a care for his life."

William's brows knitted together. "I have a care, but I also intend to make people respect me."

Broch signed. William had the same burning desire in him that Broch had, but for different reasons. As they walked, Broch lowered his voice and said, "Earning respect takes many years and can rob ye of things," Broch said, acutely aware he was now talking of himself.

William arched his brows. "What sort of things?"

"Happiness," Broch said evasively, but when William's frown deepened, Broch felt compelled to be a bit more specific. "Meaningful companionship."

A half-smile came to William's mouth. "Ye mean a woman?"

"Aye," Broch said, feeling his neck heat, but pushing forward because he was determined to warn William of what he was only just discovering about himself, and how he felt an emptiness.

William offered a dismissive wave. "I can obtain respect and a woman, if I wish."

"I fear nae," Broch said, but he knew William would not listen.

William moved closer to Broch as they walked. "I wish to train with the Dark Riders."

Broch nodded. "I thought ye might. William—"

"Ye'll nae be swaying my mind," William said vehemently, though he kept his words low.

"Then I'll nae try," Broch said, recalling how set he'd been when he'd gone, and how no one could have dissuaded him from his course. "Is that why ye came with me?"

"Aye. I figured mayhap ye would gain me entry."

"Nay," Broch said. Then when William scowled, he hastened to add, "Ye must gain it on yer own merit, but I've nae a doubt that ye will be successful." There was a fire in William and honor. Broch suspected he would become renowned in his time. "Let us see what occurs here before ye ride off into the night, aye?"

"Ye may have true need of me?" William asked.

"Aye."

"I'll nae fail ye, Broch, I vow it."

Broch clasped the other man on the shoulder as they neared the courtyard. "I did nae think ye would." And that was the true mark of honor. William would postpone his heart's desire, if Broch needed him to.

The men fell silent as they walked, and once inside the gates, Broch quickly surveyed the courtyard. It was a large rectangle with the main keep in the middle and the tall towers connecting to it by the bridges he'd noted outside the gate. The courtyard was also empty, save the warriors who guarded it.

"Are the people gathered for supper?" Broch asked, assuming the answer would be yes.

"Aye," the guard replied gruffly. "There is also a celebration of Brodee's day of birth."

Broch didn't know the day he was born, let alone the year, and he always felt a twinge of jealousy for those who did and took what they consider such a simple knowledge for granted. "How many summers is Brodee?" he asked in an effort to be polite.

"Twenty-eight this day," the man said, opening the keep door and motioning them in. Loud cheering came from a long passage, down which the guard started to lead them. When they got to the end of the hall, the guard opened a set of massive oak doors, and Broch, William, and the two Blackswells stepped into what Broch was certain was the great hall. Dinner was most assuredly over, for the tables had all been moved to the side of the hall where large, colorful tapestries hung. The tables had not been moved for dancing as often occurred at Dunvegan after dinner, but for a fight.

Broch frowned as he took in the scene. In the middle of the great hall two warriors were circling each other. They were of equal size, but it was immediately apparent that they were not of equal skill. The men were as tall as Broch and both well muscled, but the one with the red hair moved with an agility that was far greater than his opponent's. They fought with their fists, nothing more, but when the redheaded man swung his fist out in rapid-fire succession and connected with his opponent's nose, chin, then gut, Broch suspected the warrior's hands were deadly enough that he didn't often need a weapon.

The opponent doubled over, coughing, and the superior redheaded fighter yanked him up by his hair and sent a hard blow into his nose that knocked the man to the ground, unmoving. The clan roared their approval as two men scrambled to retrieve the unconscious fighter and pull him roughly to his feet as they shook him awake.

The guard beside Broch said, "Move back," and as Broch glanced around, he realized two lines of men were forming from where the warrior stood to the door that Broch had just entered. Broch and William quickly got into one of the lines just as the warrior who was jostled awake was shoved down the path the two lines created. As he staggered along, he was jeered at and men tripped him and hit him as he went until he got to the end and, passing by Broch, made his way out the door.

The great hall door slammed shut behind him, the line dispersed, and suddenly a deep voice roared, "Next!" from the dais.

Broch looked to the dais where a bear of a man stood. He had a full dark beard but a white head of hair. A long, jagged scar ran down the length of the left side of his face making him look angry, though he may well have been irritated anyway. "Is that Blackswell?" Broch asked as another man was walking toward the middle of the room where the redheaded warrior stood drinking a tankard of ale.

"Aye," the guard replied.

"What occurs here?" Broch asked.

"These men are fighting for a purse of coin that Laird Blackswell offers on Brodee's birthday every year. 'Tis more coin than most see in a year. To win it, they must defeat Brodee in one-on-one combat. If they lose, which they all do, they must walk the line of defeat. Each year Blackswell adds another purse to the one from the previous year," the guard said above the racket that surrounded them. "This has been a ritual since Brodee came into his eighteenth summer. Are ye interested in trying to win the purse?" He eyed Broch and William.

"I am," William said.

"Shut yer mouth," Broch commanded, doubting William could defeat Brodee. He was on the verge of telling the guard he was not interested either, but it occurred to him that if he won and refused the purse for himself, he could instead give it to the warriors who'd attempted to defeat Brodee and failed. The gesture would likely loosen tongues much faster than Broch attempting to gain their trust in the normal course. "If I defeat Brodee, am I at leisure to do whatever I wish with the coin?"

"Aye," the man replied. "But ye will nae defeat our captain." He smirked.

"We shall see. What do I need to do to declare my wish to be a contender?" The crowd in the great hall began to roar again, and two lines once more formed for another defeated warrior to stagger along.

In answer to Broch's question, the warrior clamped Broch's wrist and jerked his hand up in the air. When William started to withdraw his weapon and step toward Broch and the man, Broch shook his head. "Stand down. 'Tis fine."

William frowned but inclined his head and stepped back to where he had been standing.

"Laird Blackswell," the warrior clutching Broch's arm shouted above the hum of noise. "We've a new challenger for yer son, our captain, Brodee." The announcement barely got any acknowledgment the noise was so great, but the warrior was not to be waylaid. "'Tis an outsider," he shouted, his face turning red from his effort.

The noise in the great hall ceased almost immediately, save the *thunk* of the goblet Laird Blackswell had been holding being slammed upon the table. The man stood and pointed to Broch. "Ye there," he bellowed. "Name yerself."

Broch felt all eyes upon him. He jerked his wrist out of the Blackswell warrior's hold and stepped forward. "Broch MacLeod, King David's right hand. And this is my companion William MacLean, personal guard to King David."

Blackswell descended the dais surprisingly fast for a man who looked to overindulge in mead and food on a regular basis. The clap of his boots against the stone floor resounded in the now-quiet great hall. Out of the corner of his eye, Broch noticed Brodee disentangle himself from the wench who had been draped over his side, dabbing at the few cuts the Blackswell offspring looked to have sustained in his fights today. As the two men came to stand in front of Broch, he immediately disliked Brodee. The man had an arrogant smile.

"So the king's right hand wishes to fight me." The man's tone was as cocksure as his smile.

"Silence," Blackswell commanded, to which Brodee stiffened.

Blackswell had assessing blue eyes that were taking Broch's measure. The laird's gaze travelled down to where the king's ring was on Broch's hand. The man gave a nod, as if confirming Broch's words. "Why does the king send ye to us?"

"We were sent to find Katreine Kinntoch and ensure that the wedding between her and yer son go forth."

"*Were* sent to find her?" Blackswell arched his dark eyebrows.

"Aye." Broch surveyed both men as he spoke. "We already came across her in the woods near her home, close to the sea and the caves. She was defending herself against yer warriors who were attempting to ravish her. I—" William cleared his throat and gave Broch a pointed look, to which Broch had to swallow the urge to chuckle. "*We* aided her, leaving one out of three of yer warriors alive. *We* took Katreine to her home, where I told her to remain until I appraise the situation."

"Appraise—" Brodee started to growl, but Blackswell cut him off with a raised hand and a warning look.

"A wise choice," Blackswell said. "I'd nae wish the lass to come to her soon-to-be home feeling threatened. The man seemed genuine, though his son appeared greatly irritated. Maybe the laird was not the problem but the son was. Yet the son was to be Katreine's husband so it was most definitely a problem and one Broch was not as unhappy to discover as he ought to be. And he knew why. The lass was affecting him despite his determination not to allow it.

"We did send warriors to find Katreine but only because we doubted her family was truly looking for her," Blackswell said.

Broch appreciated the man's honesty. "They are hesitant," he said low, "to wed their daughter to yer son." It wasn't an outright lie, though it was a gentled version of the truth.

"I ken," Blackswell said on a sigh. "I dunnae ken of how much ye are aware, but we can discuss the particulars after the banquet, in privacy."

"A sound thought," Broch agreed.

"In the meantime," Blackswell said, waving at a guard to come forth. When the guard stood before the laird, the man ordered, "Bring Mungo to me."

The guard departed with a nod, and Blackswell turned to Broch. "I will get a full and truthful accounting of what happened, but I can assure ye, neither I nor my son would ever permit one of our men to treat a lady with anything less than respect."

Brodee nodded his agreement, though his mouth had thinned with displeasure. Broch wanted to allow his dislike to grow to a rapid hatred, but to be fair, he had to admit that the displeasure Brodee displayed could well be the result of learning one of his men had treated Katreine in a dishonorable manner.

Brodee inhaled sharply, curling his hands into fists. "My men were simply to find Katreine. I would nae ever order them to hurt her."

The man sounded heartfelt, which was good and bad

considering the pull Broch felt to Katreine. Broch nodded. "If ye dunnae mind," he said, addressing Blackswell, "I'd like to question Mungo personally." Again, William cleared his throat, but Broch gave the pup a stern look this time. Too many strangers confronting Mungo was not the way to get him to talk.

"Of course nae," Blackswell said quickly. "I would do the same if I were ye. After the fight—if ye're certain ye still wish to challenge my son—we will go to the solar and ye can question Mungo there."

"I'm always ready for a good battle," Broch said.

Blackswell chuckled. "I just need one word with my son. Fatherly advice, if ye will. I was once a great fighter, and I happen to ken that ye trained with the Dark Riders. I ken their ways, Broch MacLeod. I've seen them fight before. So I'll take a father's right to warn my son of yer talents."

Broch inclined his head as the two men moved off to the right to speak for a moment.

"What am I to do while ye question Mungo?" William whispered.

"Look around the castle for anything strange. Mayhap use yer charm to question the lasses?"

William grinned at that. "I'll be happy to."

Out of the corner of his eye, Broch saw Blackswell showing Brodee moves he thought Broch would utilize. Broch turned his back to the men. The first thing the Dark Riders had taught him was to prepare his mind for battle.

"What sort of questions should I ask the lasses?" William inquired.

Broch sighed. William was well-meaning and eager, but his timing was terrible. "Whatever comes to mind that seems as if it will reveal things we wish to ken. Now off with ye."

William gave a nod and then departed the great hall as Broch slowly stripped off his plaid so that he'd have no restrictions of his arms when he fought. He turned to see where to set it and his sword, and he found Blackswell staring at him, a look of astonishment on the man's face.

Broch frowned as Blackswell moved slowly toward him, the clanspeople gathered there parting in their laird's wake. "It kinnae be," the man said gruffly and brought his hand to Broch's shoulder. He reached out and touched the branding there. "God's teeth," Blackswell said, his voice nearly a whisper. He looked to Broch with shock-filled eyes. "Do ye ken what this is?"

Broch shook his head. "Nay. I've had it since I was a bairn. My mother—"

Blackswell gripped Broch by the shoulders. "*Where* is yer mother?"

Something in the man's voice made Broch still. "Did ye ken my mother?"

"Come with me," Blackswell said and motioned to Brodee, as well. As they made their way from the great hall, Blackswell and Brodee paused as Blackswell said something to one of his guards and the man nodded.

When Broch exited the great hall, he heard the guard call for dancing and music. Blackswell moved in front of Broch and motioned Broch to follow him as Brodee fell behind them. Broch strode behind Blackswell down a long passage filled with bustling servants and up a flight of wooden stairs to what appeared to be the laird's private solar. There were two rooms. In the room where they entered, glazed windows overlooked the courtyard. Rich tapestries depicting battle and hunting scenes hung on the walls, and there was a table and two wooden chairs with plush cushions. Broch gazed beyond the room and into the second one, which was larger and contained an enormous bed. This was definitely the laird's chamber.

He turned at the click of the door behind him and assessed Brodee.

By the frown on Brodee's face, Broch knew the man was as confused as he was. "Father, what's this about?"

Blackswell barely spared a glance for Brodee but kept his gaze mostly on Broch. "Yer mother," the man said, his voice holding an odd quiver. "Is she well?"

"She's dead." The words, though he'd spoken them often, caught in his throat as they always did. He'd not known his mother, and he was assuming the woman who had left him at Dunvegan was, indeed, his mother. But either way, she was long gone, and the knowledge always left him saddened. When Blackswell looked pained and gave him a questioning look, Broch added, "She died when I was a bairn. I dunnae remember her. I was raised by my uncle Neil."

"Yer uncle was a MacLeod?" Blackswell asked, a shadow of annoyance passing over his face. "A MacLeod!" he suddenly roared. "Of course! It all makes sense now!" The man brushed past Broch and Brodee, slung open the door, and strode out of the room, leaving Broch standing there with Brodee. The two men looked at each other but said nothing.

In moments, Blackswell returned with a MacLeod plaid in hand. He held it out to Broch. "This was yer mother's—*my wife's*."

"Yer wife?" Shock nearly knocked the breath from Broch. "If she was yer wife, then are ye—" He could not form the words. For so long he'd wondered who his father was. It was impossible that he would find the man here and now, in such a remote place and when—Devil take it, he was trying to discover if Blackswell and his son were dishonorable at best, murders at worst!

Blackswell grasped Broch by the shoulders, and a grin slowly spread across the man's face. "I'm yer father," he said, the happiness in his voice penetrating the haze that had descended on Broch.

"Father, ye kinnae ken that for certain," Brodee said. "Ye—"

"I ken it," Blackswell said, glaring at his son.

His son. The thought echoed in Broch's mind. *His son.*

Broch moved his gaze from Blackswell to Brodee, who scowled openly at him.

He is my brother? My brother, the murderer? My brother, the innocent?

There would be time enough for questions to which the answers might be painful. He flicked his attention back to Blackswell and assessed the man. He was tall, as tall as Broch. Much wider. Soft in the middle. But the eyes… God's teeth, the blue of those eyes was familiar—too familiar.

"I ken yer my son because of yer branding," Blackswell said, answering the unspoken question in Broch's mind. "I gave ye and yer brother Brodee that mark when ye were born. Ye were born on the same day with only a breath and a scream between yer births."

"What was the branding for?" Broch heard himself ask through the rushing blood in his ears. A violent storm of disbelief, gratitude, and wariness raged within him.

"The circle with the single sword through it is the symbol all future lairds of Clan Blackswell are marked with." Blackswell yanked off his plaid and pointed to his own shoulder where there was an identical branding. Broch's chest squeezed with the knowledge that what the man said was true.

"Ye are my firstborn son," Blackswell continued. "I gave ye that mark myself, just as I gave yer brother his, which shows him as the lesser son."

Broch felt his brow crease at the cold words, and his spine stiffened. He saw Brodee flinch as if he had been hit by his—no, *their*—father. Blackswell went on, oblivious. He pointed to Brodee's right shoulder. "He bears the circle but nae with the laird's sword through it. His is the dagger, the weapon that does nae hold the same weight as a sword. A sword is the weapon any warrior would always draw first."

"But a dagger," Broch said, feeling sorry for Brodee, who had turned red in the face—whether with fury or shame, Broch did not know. "A dagger is a weapon that can save yer life when a sword is too cumbersome to draw."

"A legendary fighter and a logical man!" Blackswell boomed as he slung his arm over Broch's shoulder. "*Ye* are a son I can be proud of."

God's blood! How many sleepless nights had he thought of one day meeting his father and hearing those words? But not like this, never like this. Not at the expense of his brother, whose face had drained of all color, and not without knowing for certain if his father was the man Broch had long hoped or if he was the man Katreine claimed him to be.

Christ, Katreine! She was to wed the eldest son of Blackswell, and that was now him. He highly doubted the lass would be any happier to wed him now that he was a Blackswell than she had been to wed Brodee. And how the devil could he be impartial about his own family? He glanced at Brodee and Blackswell, who were both staring at him. Brodee wore a look of hatred, which Broch could well understand given that Blackswell had basically said he was not proud of Brodee. And Blackswell wore a look of expectancy, as if—

Broch cleared his throat, realizing the man was waiting for him to say something. What to say? It all seemed unreal. He struggled to order his thoughts, then settled on one. "I think perhaps if ye could start from when ye met my mother—"

"*My* mother," Brodee growled, his eyes shooting daggers at Broch. "Nae yer mother."

"She was," Blackswell bit out and then squeezed Broch's shoulder. "Come sit here with me. We'll have some wine, and I'll tell ye all ye wish to ken."

Broch nodded and followed Blackswell to the chairs he indicated. But he realized after he sat that there were only the two chairs and that Brodee was standing there awkwardly. Why was the relationship between the two of them so strained? Broch stood and moved to sit at the fireplace ledge and motioned to Brodee. "Take this seat."

"I've better things to do than sit and hear the story of how *my* mother met *my* father. I'll go to see why Mungo is nae here yet."

"I'd still like to question him," Broch said. He looked to Blackswell, his father. Disbelief tugged at him, yet he'd seen the proof. Part of him wanted to sit and discover all he could about his mother, but he had Katreine to consider, and his loyalty to the king must come first. Yet, if he did sit with Blackswell now, perhaps the man would reveal things he may not otherwise have. Decision made, Broch said, "I can question Mungo after ye tell me of my mother."

Gratitude shone in Blackswell's eyes and tightened Broch's throat. Blackswell inclined his head toward Brodee. "We'll meet ye in the dungeon—"

"The dungeon! But we dunnae even ken if Mungo has

done these things this man says," Brodee added, pointing at Broch.

Blackswell was on his feet in a flash and toe to toe with Brodee. "This man is yer elder brother, my firstborn son. If he says Mungo was attempting to ravish the Kinntoch lass, then he was. If he's nae already in the castle, find him, seize him, and take him to the dungeon!"

Broch winced. If he and Brodee were to have any chance of an amicable relationship, he knew well from living among the four MacLeod brothers that too much rivalry between brothers bred hatred and jealousy. When one brother felt lesser in status, or even less beloved by a parent, dark emotions grew. Broch stood, trying to think how to curb Brodee's growing anger. "If ye dunnae believe my words about Mungo, Katreine Kinntoch will corroborate my story."

"Katreine would say anything to get out of wedding me," Brodee spat. "She hates all Blackswells, especially me. And now," he said, smiling maliciously, "she will hate ye, too. I kinnae say I'm pleased to have a brother, but I'm pleased nae to have to wed that hellion. Ye are the eldest," Brodee said, "and now ye will be wedding her as the king decreed. *The eldest Blackswell will wed the daughter of the Kinntoch laird to ensure peace.*" Brodee laughed. "That is, ye will wed her *if* ye can still find her when ye return for her."

Broch tugged a hand through his hair. He was in a wicked mess. If he found his clan to be innocent of the raids Katreine claimed they had been making, she'd be forced to wed him, and he her. A memory of her lush curves filled his head and stirred his desire. God's teeth, once she discovered that he was a Blackswell by birth, she'd despise him.

"Go do what ye've been ordered to do, boy," Blackswell said, his voice cold. "Yer brother and I will see ye in the dungeon."

Brodee's jaw clenched. He jerked his head in a nod and swiveled on his heel to storm from the room.

"Sit," Blackswell offered, motioning to the chair. Broch sat as Blackswell poured two goblets of wine and handed one to Broch.

The man stood there simply staring at him until Broch said, "Ye and Brodee seem to have a strained relationship."

Blackswell sighed as he sat. He crossed his legs at the ankle and gazed ahead for several silent moments. "Aye. 'Tis complicated. I suppose some of it is my fault. When yer mother fled after yer births, she took ye and left him and did nae ever return…" Blackswell shrugged, drummed his fingers on his goblet for a moment, and then took a long drink.

Broch squinted in concentration, slowly going through what he'd seen since meeting both of these men not long ago. "Do ye blame him somehow for her leaving?"

"What?" Blackswell's eyes grew wide. "Och, nay. 'Tis my fault and my fault alone that yer mother fled me. I did nae ever understand why she did nae return for Brodee, but that dunnae mean I blame him for what she did. I ken I've been hard on him, but 'tis only because I wish him to be a better man than I was at his age and nae make the same mistakes I did. But he keeps doing such damn fool things."

Broch was relieved to hear genuine affection for Brodee in Blackswell's voice, yet he suspected part of the reason Brodee kept doing "damn fool things" was because he was attempting to gain Blackswell's affection. But Broch did not feel comfortable saying such a thing. Not yet, anyway. He could not even bring himself to think of the man as his father, let alone offer advice to him on how to be a better father to Brodee.

He took a long sip of his wine, allowing the warm liquid to slide down his throat to his belly. He leaned back in his chair. "What did ye do to make my mother leave ye?"

Blackswell set down his wine goblet and leaned his forearms on his knees. He twined his fingers together and looked at Broch almost as if he were praying or kneeling to ask forgiveness. He angled his face toward Broch's, his mouth spreading into a thin-lipped smile. "I did nae banish my former mistress from the clan as yer mother demanded after we wed. I was young and prideful, and I did nae like that yer mother demanded I send my leman away. The men already teased me that yer mother had bewitched me, and truth be told, she had. I met her at the Fraser summer tourney, and she told me she was a gypsy. I was a fool and believed her. She begged me to take her with me when I left the tourney, and I did, nae ever bothering to delve into her past to learn if what she said was true." He looked down at his hands and said in a low voice, "I wanted to believe her because I wanted her, and her nae having a clan allegiance made it simple to just take her."

"She was a MacLeod," Broch said, his chest tight, hearing about his mother. Uncle Neil had said she'd been a wild one, that she had longed to be free of their parents and the marriage they had arranged for her. She must have fled with Blackswell to escape the marriage. Did he need to tell Blackswell? He glanced at the man, the stranger, his father. No, he'd not tell him. It made no difference to the man's memory of her.

"Yer mother had a temper as great as any warrior I ever kenned. She was fiercely vexed with me that I would nae banish my leman, and I became angry because she did nae trust me to nae ever touch the woman again. Then my jealous mind made me think that perhaps she did nae trust me because she had taken a lover. She became pregnant, and one night, when she would nae lie with me, I said horrid things. I—" He shook his head and looked up, pain etched on his face. "I said the wee bairns in her belly we're nae even mine. That I'd nae claim them as my heirs. She became so livid that she started having pains, and ye both came that night." Blackswell studied Broch. "Yet ye and yer brother dunnae look alike, except perhaps yer eyes. Ye both have the same eye shape yer mother possessed."

Broch imagined his mother—young, angry, prideful, and reckless—giving birth. He had never known her, but he suspected she had been much like Katreine. A strong woman. A woman who could drive a man to his knees or take him soaring to the heights of Valhalla if she chose to bestow her love upon him. "So she fled with me, thinking ye were still bedding yer leman?"

"Aye. My leman told me that her sister, Nesa, was jealous of her and likely told yer mother this to be hateful and cause trouble for her sister. Yer mother left Brodee in the care of the sister, and she left with ye two nights after ye were born."

Broch frowned. "Why only me? Why nae take Brodee, too?"

"I believe because he had developed an infection at the site of his branding. He came out weaker than ye, right from the start."

Broch scowled. Eventually, he would have to address Blackswell's treatment of Brodee. "Ye believe she left Brodee because she thought him weak?"

"Aye, because of the infection." He shrugged. "And if she could only travel with one bairn—I dunnae think she could have managed two—she naturally took ye, our firstborn son."

Broch's frown deepened. "Were ye," he started, memories of the four MacLeod brothers and how their relationships had developed and the problems they'd faced putting a question in Broch's mind. "Were ye the firstborn?"

"Nay. I was second. My brother, yer uncle Gerard, is in Valhalla," he said, looking upward to the sky where the Viking heaven was. "He was felled in battle because of a mistake I made, and I will nae ever forgive myself... I see too much of myself in yer brother."

Broch frowned at that. It seemed Blackswell feared Brodee would make the same mistakes he had made; therefore, the man was too hard on Brodee. But Broch could not yet say those things. "I think Mother did nae return because she fell ill," he said instead, thinking upon some things Neil had told him in the years gone by. "She did nae tell Neil who my father was before she died, and Neil was nae even certain she was my mother. She would nae even admit that she was."

"I ken ye dunnae recall yer mother, but did Neil tell ye what she looked like?"

Broch smiled. "He said she looked like a wee fae. She had silver-blond hair and the most unusual shade of—"

"Lavender eyes," Blackswell finished.

"Aye," Broch replied, the full realization that his father was sitting before him finally sinking in. "My mother did have eyes the color of heather."

Blackswell grinned. "'Twas what I first noticed about her. Well, that and her skill with a dagger."

An image of Katreine suddenly danced in Broch's mind, and he smiled. "There is something about a lass who can wield a dagger well, is there nae?"

"There is," Blackswell agreed, studying Broch. "Have ye met such a lass?"

He was not one to speak of personal matters to just anyone, but he had a keen desire to learn his father, to make a place in this family, and to see Blackswell's reaction to what he said. Did Blackswell hate the Kinntochs as much as they seemed to despise the Blackswells? He thought not by what Brodee had said about Katreine hating him. He'd not said he returned the dislike. "Well, I did spend a bit of time with Katreine Kinntoch, and she handles a dagger as well as any warrior I've ever seen."

Blackswell's eyes widened, and then he chuckled. "Well, as she will soon be yer wife, it's a good thing ye desire her."

"I'm nae the sort of man to force a lass to wed him," Broch said, thinking aloud.

"Nay?" Blackswell arched his eyebrows. "So as the king's right hand ye will defy him?"

"Well, nay, but—"

"Ye ken if Katreine dunnae wed ye that her family will be defying the king. They will bring his wrath upon their heads."

"Does that please ye?" Broch demanded, reminded suddenly how he really did not know this man.

"I kinnae say it would make me sad, given we would likely get all of Derthshire, but I'd hate to see the Kinntoch lose his home over his hatred for us. I feel somewhat—" Blackswell halted, looking suddenly uneasy.

"Ye feel what?" Broch prodded, sensing the man had been about to reveal something that would shed a bright light upon that which Broch sought to discover.

Blackswell stood and turned toward the door, giving his back to Broch. Was that intentional so that Broch could not read his expression? "I feel somewhat accountable," Blackswell said, his voice heavy with what sounded like regret.

"Why?" Broch asked, his heart banging. Was he about to discover that the father he'd just met was a murderer, or the brother was, or that they were indeed raiding the Kinntoch's land? And if they were, what then? Turn them in? His own family? Try to sort out the mess and see the raids stopped?

"I dunnae ken," Blackswell said after a long pause. "I suppose because I'm laird. One day when ye are laird of this clan," he said, turning toward Broch, "ye will ken what I mean. Every deed done by anyone in the clan will feel as if it is yer personal responsibility." Blackswell's eyes had a faraway look, but his face held a chasm of pain. "Come," he announced, focusing on Broch. "Let us go attend to Mungo. 'Tis one wrong we can set right."

Broch wanted to ask what the others were, but he clenched his teeth. His gut told him his father was honorable but was hiding something, holding something back. Broch would discover what, of that he was certain. What he could not say for sure is what he'd do with the information once he learned it. This morning he had been a bastard, and tonight, he wasn't. He was not keen at all to make an enemy of the family he had only just discovered. Not unless he had a true reason to.

Eight

"I did nae kill Mungo!" Brodee insisted for the second time since Broch and Blackswell had entered Mungo's cottage moments before. They'd not found Brodee or his man in the dungeon where Blackswell had ordered them to go. But they did find Mungo lying on his bed with a dagger in his neck and Brodee standing near him with blood on his plaid.

Broch glanced from Mungo to Brodee. He would have to be a fool to have killed Mungo and then stayed after doing the deed, and though Broch had not known the man long, Brodee did not seem a fool. Broch opened his mouth to say so, but Blackswell spoke first.

"Ye said the exact same thing when yer leman was killed and when Lenora was murdered," Blackswell thundered. "This is it! I'll nae hide yer misdeeds again."

Broch kept his gaze on Brodee, wanting to see his reaction. The man stiffened, and then clear hurt settled on his face. "Ye think me a murderer?" he rasped.

"I think the lasses were accidents," Blackswell said, jerking his hand through his hair. "Fit of passion with yer leman, Arabel, and an accident with Lenora. Ye argued, mayhap ye grabbed her, and she jerked away." He waved a hand in the air.

"And Mungo?" Brodee asked, his voice dead calm, like

the ocean before a violent storm. Broch recognized that restrained composure.

"He fought ye, ye got angry and reckless—"

"Christ!" Brodee spat. "Is that how poorly ye think of me? What did I ever do to ye to make ye see me thusly?" Brodee's livid gaze swung to Broch, and he pointed. "Was it because she took *him* from ye and nae me? I was the only one left, so ye settled all yer hate on me for yer own foolishness? That's what took the wife ye loved, *my mother*, from me!"

"Shut yer mouth," Blackswell bit out, and Broch heard the guilt there, as he was certain Brodee must have. He had apparently struck close to the truth.

"I did nae kill Mungo, nor Arabel, nor Lenora," Brodee said, his voice trembling with anger.

Doubt skittered across Blackswell's face. "Leave yer plaid with us and go back to the keep. Take a care to make certain ye are nae seen. Ye ken the whispers about ye already. It will only worsen if the others ken that ye were found here alone with Mungo with his blood on yer plaid."

"I did nae kill him!" Brodee thundered again. "Ye stubborn old fool! I did nae kill him, or Lenora, or Arabel, but *someone* did! Yet, instead of having the clan search for that murderer as I've told ye to for years, ye continue to order me to hide the murders ye place on my head. I'll nae do it again. I'm going to find the murderer and remove the guilt from my head."

Blackswell lunged at Brodee and grabbed him. Broch tensed, expecting Brodee to fight their father. Brodee did bring up his fist, but then he dropped his hand to his side, his shoulders sagging.

"Ye think I did nae question people?" Blackswell demanded, his tone harsh and his face going red. "Everyone I asked had seen ye with Arabel last, and then later when Lenora died, I got the same response. Ye'd been seen walking down the seagate stairs with her, for God's sake!"

"I told ye," Brodee said, shrugging away from his father, "when I left her there, she was alive. We agreed to still wed. She believed, unlike ye, that I had nae killed Arabel."

"It matters little what I believe at this point, Brodee. We lost the Derthshire land because of ye, and we need access to that land to trade with more ease. Our clan grows weak because of the dangerous route we must travel to trade with other clans. We must gain half that land again."

"I ken," Brodee said through gritted teeth.

Blackswell nodded and yanked the man to him. "It will be fine, Son," he said, affection coming through in his tone that made Broch's throat tighten. These two had many problems, but they obviously both cared for the other as father and son. Broch's own desire for such a relationship surfaced. Blackswell looked to Broch. "Katreine will surely offer less resistance to wedding Broch than ye, so the wedding can take place immediately. Then we will gain half of Derthshire." Blackswell gave Broch an appealing look. "Ye will wed the lass, aye?"

Broch shifted uncomfortably. Devil take it. He hated having to tell them what he'd promised, but he had to keep his vow. He quickly told them of his pledge to Katreine and her family to question the Blackswell clan—*his clan*—and discover if they had been raiding the Kinntoch land. He also mentioned that if they had, the Blackswells would be forced to forfeit any claim to Derthshire, per the king's dictate.

"If I find that yer clan is innocent, I'll do my duty as yer eldest son." He inhaled a long, deep breath, considering that soon he may be wedding Katreine, who undoubtedly would not like it, as he was now a Blackswell.

"Ye mean if ye find *our* clan innocent, aye?" Brodee clarified, smirking. "Surely the favored son, the eldest son"—Brodee's gaze flicked to Blackswell—"would nae betray his own clan. I ken I'd die before doing so."

Blackswell and Brodee stared at Broch. "I would nae ever wish to betray the clan, but I'd nae lie—"

"It dunnae matter," Blackswell said, waving his hand. "We have nae raided the Kinntoch land, so ye will nae find a thing. Brodee will personally take ye to question clan members on the morrow. Now make haste away, Brodee. Broch and I will deal with Mungo."

Later that night, Broch stood over Mungo's grave, which he and Blackswell had dug together. Broch said a quick prayer for the man's damned soul, for he did nae think a man who would abuse a woman had a place in Valhalla.

He turned to Blackswell who had been quiet since Brodee had departed. "Tomorrow, when I'm questioning the clan about the raids, I'll also make inquiries regarding the murders."

"I fear ye will receive the same answers I did when I made inquiries. Brodee was the last person seen with Arabel and with Lenora, and if ye tell all in the clan that Mungo was also murdered, word will travel to the Kinntochs and that will be one more reason the laird will nae wed his daughter to ye. It's better ye are wed before we announce that Mungo was murdered. Mayhap ye could make yer inquiries about the raids quickly, and once ye are wed, we can hunt Mungo's murderer?"

Broch frowned. "But that leaves the murderer running around, and—"

"For a day, at most," Blackswell said. "Ye can spend all day tomorrow questioning everyone ye wish, and if ye hear enough to believe us innocent, ye can collect yer bride the next day and be wed that night. Once ye're wed and she's publicly bedded—"

"Nay," Broch said, always having hated that practice. "My word will have to be sufficient."

Blackswell inclined his head and cleared his throat. "Once the marriage is sealed, I'll personally question everyone with ye. Think ye I want to believe Brodee a murderer?"

"Nay," Broch said, seeing it in his pleading eyes.

"All will be well," Blackswell pronounced. "Now that ye have been returned to me, all will be well."

It felt as if a boulder had been placed on Broch's shoulders. He wanted to secure a place in his new family, ease the tension he'd found here, and help them secure their half of Derthshire, but he could not do so at any price. He would complete a thorough investigation, albeit a quick one. That, he could do. And if he found they were innocent, which he prayed he would, he would go to collect Katreine and persuade her to do as the king had decreed. Guilt niggled at him knowing she would have no choice but to wed him or allow her family to suffer the king's wrath, but he could not control what the king would do.

Besides, he and Katreine already desired each other, so surely, if they did end up wedding, she would accept him, and then he would have the family he had long ago wished for but had given up on.

A sennight after Broch had departed without so much as a

farewell, Katreine was swimming in the loch, trying to enjoy the sunshine and put thoughts of the blue-eyed devil out of her mind. But no matter how hard she tried to stop her mind from roaming to Broch, it did so every single day. What was he doing? Had he finished his investigation? Surely, he'd discovered her family was correct about the Blackswells. Maybe, he'd sent word to the king already and would be returning here soon to tell her she did not have to marry into that dreadful family.

Hope flared at the thought. If she was free, the future was open before her. The ability to wed for love, a longing she had secretly harbored with the hundreds of recollections of watching her parents together and very much in love, would become a real possibility. Maybe Broch would even be the man she chose. The fact that it would be *her choice* was very important to her.

She thought of the promise she had made her mother right before her mother had died...

The salty breeze blew in from the ocean as Katreine sat on the beach with her mother. She stole a sideways glance at her, and her breath caught in her throat. Her mother was so very frail looking. Suddenly, she turned to Katreine and took her hand. "I have made yer father vow to me that ye will be able to wed for love. We pushed Lenora toward Brodee before she even kenned him, and look what happened to her in the end. Ye must come to truly ken the man ye think ye will wed, as I kenned in my heart that yer father was good, honorable, and true. Vow this to me, Kat."

"I vow it, Mama," she said.

As the memory faded, Katreine flipped onto her back and closed her eyes, but the minute she started to feel light in the water, the sound of the war horn being blown ripped through the silence. God's teeth! Without hesitation, she turned onto her belly and started swimming to the shore, pushing her legs and arms as fast as they would go. Her lungs burned and her side cramped as she scrambled onto the beach, grasped her dagger that was lying on her clothes, and snatched up her gown. She did not bother with her slippers.

She raced through the woods toward her home, tugging on her gown as she went while gripping her dagger. When she reached where the forest met the road, she gasped at the sight of hundreds of Blackswell warriors on warhorses, approaching her home in two long lines from the left. The drawbridge to the castle was up, and from the other side, in the safety of the inner keep, the thundering of her clan's own warhorses resounded in the night.

Even if she ran toward the gate, she feared the approaching Blackswells would simply run her down, but she could not hide and do nothing as her family possibly engaged in battle. Had the Blackswells decided war between the clans was inevitable? She could not believe they were willing to give up their half of Derthshire by fighting her family. Where was Broch? Maybe he'd talked reason into them, but if so, then why were so many warriors here? Dear God, had they harmed Broch?

She looked to the right and thought. If she picked her way through the woods, she could make it to the bridge and jump into the moat. Her family would throw a rope to get her out. Decision made, she turned toward her home, but as she did, a stick snapped behind her and she was grabbed. She twisted away, losing her balance and her dagger in the process, and she fell through the branches onto the dirt road. A horse neighed loudly, and all she saw was the blur of hooves as the horse reared onto its hind legs, so near her face that she felt the push of air.

When she looked up and over her right shoulder, a

powerful black destrier loomed above her with his hooves kicking at the air. "God above!" a voice yelled, and then the destrier's feet swooped down so close to her that for a moment, her gown was pinned under a hoof. When the horse neighed again and danced backward, she scrambled to her knees to grasp her dagger she'd dropped, but before she could gain her feet, hands came under her arms and she was pulled up to standing.

She looked up and met Broch's incredulous face. His eyes seemed to glow with fear which turned swiftly to anger as he stared at her. "Ye," he said, his voice a rumble of restrained power. "Ye..." He swept his gaze over the length of her body, and she had the oddest notion he was assuring himself that she was not harmed. When his stance seemed to relax, she was almost certain of it, and a bubble of joy expanded in her chest. "Ye," he said again, "are either a fool or ye're unaccountably reckless."

She was so glad to see him here and alive that without thought, she hugged him and said, "I'm unaccountably reckless."

His hand came to her hair, and he pushed it off one shoulder and over her ear while he leaned close. His lips grazed her lobe. "I like a reckless lass," he whispered, his warm breath fanning her sensitive skin.

She shivered with a sharp pull of desire, and then someone cleared their throat and she remembered in a flash that she was standing in the middle of the road with the Blackswells pressing down on her family. She turned, knowing the Blackswell army was there before her, and squared her shoulders.

The first person she saw was William, Broch's companion, at whom she smiled, but then she saw Brodee sitting on his horse so smugly beside his father's. Behind them by ten paces, their warriors had halted. She tilted up her chin. "It will do ye no good now to try to snatch me and force me to wed ye, Brodee Blackswell," she spat. "Ye have broken the king's edict by marching here to start a war with my family."

An amused look skittered across the man's face, taking Katreine by surprise. A piece of white cloth tied to a stick was dangled in her face as Brodee leaned forward. "We've nae broken any edict, lass," he said. She had a hard time tearing her disbelieving gaze away from the white cloth.

"Ye are nae here to force me to wed ye, either?"

"Nay. We're here for ye to wed my brother," he said, his gaze becoming intense and moving to Broch, who stiffened behind her. She glanced over her shoulder, only just realizing Broch had positioned himself directly behind her and had drawn his sword. She gave him a smile, appreciative beyond words that he would risk himself for her, but then she turned to face Brodee and Laird Blackswell once more. Behind her, she heard the drawbridge creaking as it lowered.

"Hold up the peace flags," Broch commanded, and to her shock, Brodee did as Broch ordered and held the flag high.

A hundred questions flew through her mind. "What brother?" she demanded of Brodee. "Ye dunnae have one. What trickery is this? What lies have ye told Broch?" She was sure they must have fed him nothing but untruths and now they'd drawn him here. What was their plan?

"Brodee," Broch said, his voice a lethal warning.

The look of hatred that settled on Brodee's features as he stared at Broch made gooseflesh sweep Katreine's arms.

"Aye, Brother?" Brodee snarled.

"Brother?" Katreine repeated, looking back at Broch in

disbelief. That could not be so! Broch was a MacLeod, not a—She gasped as the possibility, the awful possibility, sunk in. He had said himself he did not know who his father was. "No!" she burst out, feeling as if her hope for the future was slipping away before she'd ever had a chance to see if it was real.

"Katreine," Broch said gently, pain in his voice. *The pain of the truth.* She clenched her teeth on a scream as horses' hooves pounded toward them. She turned fully to Broch. Maybe even if he had discovered impossibly that he was the son of Blackswell, he was still honorable as she had first thought.

"Tell me," she implored him, locking her gaze with his. "Tell me ye have uncovered the truth as I told ye. Tell me ye are nae here to force me to wed ye. Tell me ye have nae become a Blackswell in spirit, as well as name, in one short sennight."

The frustrated look he gave her said it all, but devil take the man, he spoke anyway, making her heart squeeze into a tight little ball of sorrow for what might have been. "They are nae raiding yer land, Katreine. They are innocent; therefore, I kinnae write to the king on yer behalf."

"I will nae wed ye…ye Blackswell!" she hissed, turning on her heel with a thundering heart to rush toward her father and her brothers, who were approaching. She was halted by an iron grip to her wrist. She turned toward Broch, intent on flaying him with words, but he stepped to her, cupped her neck, and brought their faces a hairsbreadth apart.

"Ye can refuse to wed me," Broch said, "but if ye do, ye will be responsible for yer family losing Derthshire and possibly much more. The king is a fair man, but he is nae a forgiving man when one of his subjects disobeys his rulings.

It may be that he simply takes Derthshire away from yer family. It may be that he takes the castle. It may be that he demands a life—mayhap nae yers but mayhap one of yer brothers or yer father."

Katreine shuddered inwardly at the possibility.

"Katreine?" her father said over her shoulder, so that she knew her family had reached them.

"Release my sister, MacLeod!" Donell yelled.

Broch's gaze flicked over her shoulder for one moment, his face becoming implacable, his eyes steely. "If yer sister demands it, I will," he assured Donell in a calm but firm tone.

As indecision warred within her, Katreine bit her lip until it throbbed as powerfully as her pulse. Behind her, the thud of boots hitting earth alerted her to the fact that her father or one of her brothers had dismounted. Her time to decide was almost up. They would do everything to protect her from having to marry into the Blackswells, even sacrifice themselves. She could not allow that.

She looked at the face of the man who would be her husband, a man who thoughts of had once filled her with promise. She felt as if she had somehow been duped. Sunlight glimmered over his perfectly rugged features like beams of icy radiance. She'd let her guard down like a fool for a handsome face. No, a wickedly beautiful face, damn the Scot. She might have to wed Broch to save her family, but she would not go like a meek, foolish little lamb to be slaughtered. She was a shield-maiden!

"I will wed ye," she said, her thoughts turning at a dizzying rate, sorting possible plans, discarding them, and then settling on one. "I will do it to save my family, but I will nae ever"—she lowered her voice to a whisper—"surrender my body, nor my heart to ye, ye baseborn bastard."

The gentleness that had been in his eyes disappeared, as if someone had obliterated the emotion from his soul. She sucked in a sharp breath, the words she'd just spoken echoing in her ears, her mind, the very chambers of her heart. Her anger boiled within her, yet she felt the slightest niggle of guilt for the horrible thing she'd said, and it deepened when she saw the cold fury that turned his eyes a frigid shade of blue. His jaw tensed, and his pulse was noticeable at his neck.

She was suddenly acutely aware of her father and brothers standing behind her and William, Blackswell, and Brodee still seated on their warhorses behind Broch. She'd shamed him, she was certain. The fury in his eyes disappeared as quickly as the gentleness had, and a cold dignity created a stony mask on his face. He gave her a bland smile. "I'm nae a bastard, Hellion. My parents were wed when they conceived me."

Shame seared her from the inside, but she held her tongue and tilted her chin higher, refusing to retract her words.

His lips drew into a hard line, then he inhaled slowly, and said, "And just so ye understand me, I dunnae have a use for yer heart, but I'm afraid I must insist ye give me yer body, at least once, to seal our marriage vows."

Nine

Broch had never thought upon the day he would wed, but he felt certain that if he had mused over it, the day would not have included him being surrounded on either side by angry men with drawn swords. Nor would it have included a bride-to-be who kept shooting him scathing looks and stood stiff as a board by his side.

When he saw her tremble, he considered offering her a reassuring touch, perhaps a brush of his fingers to her small, pale ones, but he knew well she'd not welcome the gesture. A hot flash of anger shot through him again at the memory of her derisive comment not long ago. Yet when he stole a sideways glance at her, this delicate lass so full of pride who was about to become his wife—*his wife*—the last lingering bits of his anger faded away, and bitter regret for the clotheid way he'd reacted to her remarks assailed him.

There were a hundred—no, a thousand—ways he could have handled that better and shown her understanding instead of anger. If he had chosen even one of those options, perhaps she'd not look like a hunted doe now. As the priest, who her brother had gone to fetch after everyone had finished yelling and Broch had explained the situation, entered the room and walked toward them holding the cords he would use to bind their hands, Broch felt Katreine's slight trembling become much more pronounced.

"We'll start with the traditional wedding prayer," the ruddy-faced priest announced.

"Tradition," Katreine blurted, her eyes bright with fear. "We must adhere to tradition!" She turned fully to face Broch now. "I kinnae wed ye unless we adhere to the tradition of the Kinntoch clan. It would be ill luck!"

The desperation in her voice made his chest squeeze, and he knew then and there that he'd follow whatever ritual she needed him to. "What tradition do ye wish us to abide?"

The priest waved a hand at them. "Dunnae fash yerself about any traditions, lass. The Lord dunnae care—"

"Please, Father Randalf, do hold yer tongue," she interrupted.

Father Randalf gasped at Katreine, eliciting a momentary contrite look upon her breathtakingly beautiful face. "I am sorry, Father," she said, her voice like honey. A genuinely apologetic smile graced her features before lines of determination settled between her brows. Broch's instincts tightened within him. Katreine was stirring sort of mischief, and he had no doubt it was aimed at him. Whether it was to stall the inevitable wedding or to strike at him, he did not know, but this time, he would handle whatever Katreine did or said with more understanding and a restrained tongue.

"Have ye come to yer senses, then, lass?" the Kinntoch asked.

Broch tensed when she started to nod in agreement, but then she caught herself and shook her head. "I wish the wedding to proceed," she said, her tone underlain with obvious strain, "but we must adhere to tradition."

"What tradition?" her father asked, his brow creasing.

Donell strolled to her side, glaring at Broch, and then her brother slung an arm around Katreine. "Ye ken the tradition, Da. The long-standing one of the Blackening of the Groom."

Her father's frown deepened, revealing the obvious: there was no such tradition. Broch watched as Katreine's eyes lit with hope, and in that moment, Broch realized she was so desperate not to wed him that she had blurted this likely in the hope that her father would rescue her. But she would not ask him to do so. Never would the proud lass ask such a thing. Admiration for her strength and bravery pulsed in him. He studied her father. What would the man do? Broch didn't know whether he'd be angrier if her father called off the wedding and made himself and Katreine an enemy of the king or if her father did nothing and knowingly allowed her to sacrifice herself for the good of the Kinntoch clan.

"Oh aye!" her father exclaimed. "Of course. The Blackening of the Groom." Kinntoch's eyes flashed with ire as they settled on Broch. "I'm old, ye see. Sometimes I need a moment for my memory to take hold."

Broch swallowed the curses he wanted to hurl at the man for not protecting his daughter no matter what, however foolish and unwise that was. And it was. The man had most definitely made the wise choice for the clan, but Broch could not help but think of the hurt Katreine must be feeling, considering she was sacrificing herself for her clan's welfare. Had she had a secret hope her father would somehow rescue her?

"Ye'll nae blacken my firstborn!" Blackswell objected.

"Tradition must be observed," Kinntoch growled.

"Or the marriage will nae produce bairns," Donell offered, smirking.

"Well," Blackswell spat, "if we must observe that tradition, then the bride should be blackened, too."

Katreine dismissed the hurt she was feeling at her father's apparent ease in sacrificing her for the clan. It was how it should be, even though it meant she was soon to be wed. Heaven above! She sneaked a look at Broch, face set in brooding lines, and she cringed. Why had she allowed herself to become so desperate that she'd lied about a tradition needing to be observed before they wed? She grasped at the material of her skirts with sweaty palms. She could not recant her words, for the Blackswell men—who now included Broch, she thought dismally—would know she'd fibbed.

Her heart raced as she thought of the Blackening ritual that many clans in these parts followed. Hers never had, and if she was lucky, they would only strip her to her léine and not completely naked, as she had seen done before. Then they would spread hive honey all over her and feathers, and then… She swallowed past the lump in her throat. Then they would parade her through the castle and his clan, the Blackswells, would make crude remarks and ogle her while her clan would shame him. God's teeth, she was a fool. She wanted to protest, yet pride kept the objection from escaping.

"Nay," Broch said, responding to his father in such a chilling voice that Katreine felt her jaw slip open, even as gratefulness enshrouded her.

"But, Son," Blackswell started to protest, but Broch gave him such a dark look that the man, to Katreine's amazement, fell silent.

"I will nae have Katreine paraded through the castle for all to see." His eyes locked on hers, the intensity in them making her shiver. "I will nae have another man looking upon what is only mine to look upon from this day forward."

It was a declaration to her and to all who were present in the great hall, which included her father and brothers, and Broch's father and brother, as well as the priest and five warriors from each clan. She inhaled a sharp breath to protest being claimed so, but then she clamped her jaw shut, relief flooding her. Broch had offered her a way out of the folly she'd created, and she would gladly take it, but what of him? She could not allow him to be shamed because of her doing, no matter how angry she was, no matter how much she did not want to wed him, *a Blackswell*.

"Mayhap," she said, drawing in a shaky breath, "since the wedding is to happen with such haste, the tradition can be omitted?"

"Nay," her father and Donell said at once. Her brother's accusing gaze, a gaze that warned her not to betray her clan, burned into her. "If the Blackswell bastard—"

"Donell!" she gasped, looking to Broch and seeing no indication the slur had bothered him other than the tic that was barely noticeable at his right eye.

"My son was nae born a bastard," Blackswell growled and reached for his sword, but Broch, to Katreine's relief, shook his head at his father.

"Nay," he said, his attention never straying from her. "I'll nae have bloodshed the day I wed. I've been called much worse than a bastard in my lifetime, so dunnae take offense on my account. Let us get on with the ritual. I would be wed this night."

And without blinking an eye, his gaze boring into her, he offered his sword to his father to hold, and in utter silence, he stripped off his plaid, then spread his arms wide. Her mouth went dry, and her pulse spiked. His skin glowed bronze, his chest was slabs of muscles layered upon each other. His shoulders were wide and appeared as if they could bear the needs of many, and his arms, flexed as they were, made his muscles bulge and her stomach tighten. She sucked in a breath. That same treacherous desire that had drawn her to him the last time they were together was still so powerful within her, even knowing he was forcing her to wed into his despicable family. Maybe he'd known he was a Blackswell all along and had simply been toying with her.

No, that was ridiculous. Broch had killed Blackswell warriors. He would not have done such a thing if he had known he was one of them. Still, Broch must have gotten to the Blackswell, discovered who he was, and decided to betray her. As she looked at him standing there, so powerful, so dangerously enticing, she became angry all over again.

He arched his eyebrows and an amused look, as if he knew she was fighting her desire for him, turned up the corners of his mouth. "Is this bare enough for ye, Katreine? Will this satisfy the tradition so that we ensure our joining will bear fruit in yer womb?"

She could not conjure a quick scathing reply, let alone could her mouth form the words. Instead, her weak mind fabricated a picture of her in his arms, his lips on hers, and the feelings of blissful pleasure he had given her in their one, brief, passionate encounter. His smile grew wider, and she glared at him. Oh, the devil Scot! He knew what she was thinking.

"'Tis nae enough," Donell said. "Ye must strip all the way."

Katreine felt her jaw drop at those words. She looked to her father, but he seemed well pleased. Even Broch's own brother, the murdering Brodee, seemed to have a look of eager anticipation on his face for the shame that awaited his brother. Only William, Blackswell, and his warriors looked angry, but Broch shook his head at his father and William, a subtle warning not to interfere. What was he trying to prove? That nothing they could do to him would shame him? That they could not win? Or was it something else? Something she was missing?

"Is that what ye need, Katreine? For the tradition to be fully met? Do ye need me to strip bare?"

There it was again. The indefinable emotion in his eyes, and yet…and yet she thought he was trying to offer her something. An olive branch, perhaps? A chance for them not to hate each other? There was a small part of her, the part that could recall the kiss and how she had felt after, that hoped there might be something between them, that wanted to take the offer he was extending to her. But then she recalled her dead sister and her mother, who passed in heartbreak soon after, all because of the Blackswells. And she thought upon the raids they'd been enduring, and she pulled the fading edges of her anger around her to cloak herself in it.

"Aye," she said, and in her mind, she heard the branch he'd held out to her snap. His eyes grew hard, but they were no longer on her. They were locked upon Donell, whose face was twisted with his hatred of Broch, whom he barely knew—except, of course, that he was a Blackswell.

The great hall door swung open, and Cadyn rushed in holding honey and feathers. Katreine blinked, not even realizing Cadyn had departed. He raced toward their father and held out the supplies, but he offered an apologetic look to Broch, a look that made Katreine feel the sharp bite of guilt for a brief moment. Her brother seemed able to look past the fact that Broch was a Blackswell now, though she could not?

"To bind our clans," her father said, "because we have been bitter enemies, it is my belief that the Blackening should be a Strike Blackening."

Katreine recoiled at her father's words. It was one thing to shame Broch, but she would not stand quietly and say nothing at her father's proposal that Broch walk the castle bridge naked, covered in honey and feathers, and be struck by the warriors of her clan."

"Father—"

"Silence, Katreine," her father said coldly.

Blackswell smacked a fist into his open palm, his face near purple. "My son will nae—"

"I will," Broch said, shocking her from her scalp to her toes. "If this will truly settle the feud between the two clans, I will submit to it."

"It will," her father said. But something in his voice and in his eyes told her otherwise.

"Father, a word," she interrupted again.

He did not acknowledge her. Instead, he said to Broch, "Strip."

Broch's eyes narrowed upon her father. "Yer daughter spoke to ye," he said, his tone biting.

Her eyes went wide. Broch was standing up for her.

"Daughter?" Her father motioned for her to follow him. She had little choice but to scramble out of the great hall behind him, but as she passed Broch, she could feel his eyes on her.

When the door to the hall closed behind them, and they stood in the passage alone, her father faced her, an irritated expression on his face. "Why did ye interrupt?"

"Do ye speak the truth that this will end the feud? As much as I hate the Blackswells, I dunnae wish to see Broch harmed."

"Ye dunnae believe yer sister deserves vengeance?" he bit out.

His harsh words hurt her. "Aye, but—"

"Good." He hugged her to him, then drew her away and grasped her shoulders. "Let us return—"

"Father, the men will hurt him." It was one thing for her to plan to somehow get him to send her back home to live after they were wed, but it was another thing to knowingly allow him to be injured because of her. They—"

"Nay. Dunnae fash yerself. I will instruct them to strike with a verra restrained hand. This is symbolic, Katreine. Broch knows this or he would nae have agreed to it. Ye think him a fool?"

"Nay." She didn't know what to think about him.

"Go ring the bell and gather the clan to the bridge. I'll send Cadyn to aid ye. Donell, Lannrick, and I will prepare Broch and bring him to make the walk down the bridge with the others."

She stood there, not wanting to go but feeling she had no choice but to do as he bade. After a long moment, she inclined her head, and her father left her standing there. She got no more than ten steps when footfalls echoed behind her. When she turned, Cadyn was there, frowning at her.

"What?" she snapped, her guilt making her terse.

"I hope ye can live with whatever happens."

She clenched her jaw on a spike of fear. "Father says it will be a symbolic striking."

"Do ye believe Father will stand idly by and let them have ye and the land? Nay, he's out for blood, and ye just served yer future husband to Father on a trencher."

Fear chilled her heart. She started to push past her brother to go back to the great hall, but Cadyn grabbed her wrist. "Release me," she demanded.

"Nay, Katreine. 'Tis too late to stop it now. The man ye are wedding is a legendary warrior. He'll nae retreat from that to which he committed. It would make him look weak."

She bit hard on her lip as she thought. Despite the little amount of time she'd spent with Broch, she'd seen enough to know his reputation as a ferocious, undefeatable warrior had been well-earned. Cadyn was correct. It was very unlikely that Broch would not go through with the Blackening ritual now. It would make him look weak in the eyes of her clan, as well as his. Her chest squeezed so tightly she could barely take a breath. She hated the Blackswells, but that did not mean she wanted to see Broch hurt. Yet Cadyn was correct: she'd offered up the man she would soon be bound to for the foreseeable future. What would he do in retaliation? The thought made her shiver.

Ten

She wanted to look away, but she couldn't. Broch stepped onto the bridge at the opposite end, and her clan began to chant, "Walk. Walk. Walk."

Even stripped naked and covered as he was in honey and feathers, he carried himself with a commanding air of self-confidence. Every inch of his body exuded raw power as he began the journey down the bridge. Two steps in and the first fist flew to strike Broch's back from one of her family's warriors. She winced but forced herself to watch what was her fault. She blew out a relieved breath that Broch did not seem affected, so the blows, as they started to come from the left and right had to be soft, as her father had promised they would be.

Still, her heartbeat increased with each step he took and every blow he received. Pain shot through her jaw, and she forced herself to unclench her teeth, but just as she did, Donell struck such a blow to Broch on the back of his neck that he staggered forward. She cried out, covering her mouth with her hand when Broch glanced toward her, only to be struck again in the same spot by a warrior from Donell's personal command.

She scanned the distance he had left to the end of the bridge—ten steps perhaps. Dear God above, would he make it? Her nails dug into the flesh of her palms, cutting the skin, yet she could not make herself unclench her hands. Nine steps. Another blow came, and she jerked out of her place in the line, only to be tugged back by Cadyn and Lannrick.

"'Tis almost over," Cadyn said, to which Lannrick nodded.

Two more steps and what seemed like countless blows came. Broch staggered again, yet kept moving forward like an invincible force. But of course, he was vulnerable. He was just a man, no matter the legend.

"Look away," Lannrick said when she whimpered as Broch slowed to nearly a stop under a deluge of blows.

Each impact resounded in her ears. She shook her head as tears for him filled her eyes. Finally, he stepped off the bridge and walked to where she stood with Lannrick, her father, and Cadyn. A wave of guilt like she'd never known assailed her as the tall Scot came to stand before her, bloody and naked.

"I'm sorry!" she blurted, wanting to drop to her knees before him and beg him to forgive her. "I'm so verra sorry."

She tensed as his gaze settled on her, but then he gave her a smile that seemed without malice. He closed the distance between them and ran his fingers down her cheek. "I hold that apology dear coming from such a proud lass as yerself," he said to her amazement. "Let us put this and the hatred between our clans behind us now and be wed."

Without thought, she nodded, only realizing what she'd done when her father clamped a hand on her arm and squeezed. She immediately stilled, but Broch's eyes glowed with triumph, which made her feel like a traitor to her clan. Why had she nodded? She could not deny that in that moment, she had wanted to put it all behind them, as he had suggested.

Before she could contemplate it further, her father

growled, "Clean up. We will see ye shortly in the great hall. Come, boys!" he commanded of her brothers, then practically dragged her to the great hall and slammed the door behind her.

"Ye kinnae relent to Broch!" he father roared.

She was glad no one was in the great hall but her and her brothers. Heat infused her face. "I will nae. I—"

"Ye nodded!" Father accused.

She had, and she had no words to defend herself.

"Ye nodded when he suggested we put the murder of yer sister behind us. The Blackswells are liars."

"Ye lied!" she burst out. "Ye told me the blows would nae be harsh!"

"I did nae lie!" her father roared. "Donell disobeyed my orders, and he will be punished. If ye relent to Broch, if ye become a Blackswell in heart as well as in name, it will be disloyal to our clan and to the memory of yer dead sister! And yer mother, as well!" he finished, his voice shaking. "Ye kinnae relent and accept being a member of the clan that protects the man who killed yer sister!"

She knew she should say she would not, and before Broch had walked that bridge, she'd have said it, but his words about peace echoed in her ears and her heart. Cadyn's words about not judging Broch until he's proved to be like his clan replayed in her mind, as well. "Father—"

"Nay!" He held up his hand to silence her. "Mark me, Daughter. That man kens his family is evil. He chose to overlook it and side with them when he discovered he was a Blackswell. There is loyalty in that, aye. I give him that. But by choosing to ignore the foul deeds against our family—the murder, the raids—he has chosen to be our enemy. He kenned that. He had to. And he made the choice anyway. Now ye must choose. Will it be loyalty to the man ye will take as husband or loyalty to us? Choose now!"

Broch stood outside the closed doors of the great hall in his plaid and braies, still dripping with water from his quick washing. Beside him was his father, Brodee, Father Randalf, and William. Broch stilled, hearing Kinntoch roaring inside the great hall, each word utterly clear. His breath quickened in anticipation of how Katreine would answer the demand to decide her loyalty.

"Loyalty to my family, Father," she finally said.

"I'd nae wed that lass if I were ye," William said.

"Ye're nae me," Broch snapped.

Despite her words, he'd noted the hesitation, just as he noted earlier the real sorrow and despair in her voice for her part in the Blackening. That proud lass wanted to forgive whether she knew it yet or not, and he was not one to turn away from a challenge. He never had been, and she was likely the biggest challenge he'd ever encountered.

"Ye kinnae withdraw from the wedding," his father said.

Broch glanced at him. The man had mistaken Broch's not barging into the great hall for him having misgivings about doing his part. But he was not questioning his decision. Initially, he had thought he had agreed to the wedding for two reasons: he did not want to fail his new family and be undeserving of a place in it, and he had told himself he was helping Katreine, whether she knew it or not, by giving her family a chance to keep their land. But the minute he'd seen her again, he'd known there was a third reason he could not ignore: he desired her. And it was his desire for her that had been the final persuading factor, which he had refused to acknowledge until now. He could not, in truth, deny it. He wanted to win her loyalty. He wanted to make her *want* to be his. And he suspected the best way to do that was with patience.

God help him, he hoped he had enough.

The wedding took place so quickly that Katreine would have thought she dreamed it if she were not being lifted by Broch—her husband—upon his warhorse. Tears blurred her eyes as he turned his destrier to fall in line with his family—the treacherous Blackswells.

She was keenly aware of the powerful thighs pressed upon either side of her own. His hard chest brushed her back, despite the fact that she'd tried to scoot forward enough to put distance between them, and his thick, corded arms braced her as he held the reins of his beast.

She wanted to hate him as she was supposed to. Instead, she kept thinking of the wedding ceremony and the smile that had turned up his mouth as he'd stared unwaveringly at her, and the merriment in his eyes, even when she had boldly taken untraditional vows and said, *Ye cannot possess me, for I belong to myself, Ye cannot command me, for I am my own person.*

His response replayed in her mind, and she found herself smiling: *I shall serve ye in the way ye require, and the honeycomb shall taste sweeter coming from my hand.*

She really had to work harder to remember she was expected to dislike him. He was a Blackswell, after all, and she had vowed to her father that she would not relent to him.

"Are ye cold, lass?" he asked, and his arms seemed to move closer to her body.

She jabbed him with her elbow. "Of course I'm cold, ye clot-heid. Wedding ye has chilled me to the bone." There, let him do what he would with that.

Behind their destrier came a hearty chuckle.

Broch pulled his destrier to a halt, and those behind them simply maneuvered their horses around them on the path and kept riding, not daring to glance at them. All of them except William. She suspected the others feared Broch, but William seemed to be trying to pattern himself after her new, ill-begotten husband. She wanted to find fault with William for it, but she could not. Broch seemed rather invincible to her, as well. Even after all the blows he had taken from her family, he had not seemed the least inhibited by pain. She didn't understand it, but she was secretly glad of it, for him.

"William, if ye wish to make yer way to yer final destination, ye have my leave."

Katreine's lips parted. Was he banishing him for laughing?

William's eyebrows arched. "Ye're certain?"

A genuine smile graced Broch's lips. "Aye. I'll have two Blackswell warriors tend to the birlinn. Ye need nae fash yerself. I'll send word to the MacLean and the king of yer whereabouts, but I will give ye this parting advice: being a legend will nae satisfy whatever is empty within ye."

Was Broch speaking of himself? He had to be. She feared his need to prove he deserved a place in his clan had been transferred to the Blackswells.

She cleared her throat, intent on offering William her own advice. "Dunnae seek to be a legend at all. Seek to be honorable."

"I plan to be both, just like Broch," William said, giving her a pointed look before he turned his horse out of the line.

He disappeared into the woods.

As she mulled over William's words, Broch shifted behind her, and then his plaid, which he'd been wearing, settled on her shoulders. Strong, quick, sure hands began to tuck the soft fabric around her. His fingers grazed her breasts, then her waist, and finally her bottom. She was stunned into stillness by surprise and a searing jolt of wantonness. Devil take the man, her body responded to his, despite her mind telling it not to.

"Stop it," she said finally, managing to slap behind her.

He caught her hand and pressed a kiss to her fingertips, which sent prickles all the way up her arm. "Yer wish is my command."

"Aye?" she asked. "Then I command ye to turn around yer beast and take me home."

"I'm taking ye home, lass," he said with irritating gentleness. "To yer new home. Our home."

He sounded so proud that she considered for a moment, letting him have this one victory, for she knew what it likely meant to him to have a home that was truly his, considering he had thought himself a bastard, but then she recalled her vow to her father. "'Tis nae my home," she growled. He sighed. Feeling a wiggle of guilt, she asked, "How did ye come to discover Blackswell was yer father?"

Broch's arms settled once more on either side of her, and after giving a command to his horse for it to move, he said, "When I first arrived there, I thought to fight Brodee to win a purse of money that I intended to use to loosen the Blackswells' tongues to get the answers I promised I'd seek for ye." She snorted at that but held her comment, wishing to hear how he'd discovered he was a Blackswell. "When I took off my plaid, Blackswell—"

"Dunnae ye mean yer father?" she asked sarcastically.

Och! Why had she not kept her mouth closed?

"I kinnae bring myself to call him such yet. Mayhap I nae ever will."

"Nay?" she snapped. "But ye took their side so easily and did nae bother to do as ye promised me!"

"I did, Katreine," he said in a gentle voice. "I inquired for a full sennight. I spoke with over two hundred Blackswell clan members, and nae a one kenned anything of raids upon yer clan or even a whisper of a Blackswell doing something they ought nae to do."

She snorted. "Ye heard what ye wished to hear."

"I heard what they told me," he corrected. "And I discerned the truth of their words in their eyes."

"Because ye wanted it to be true," she growled.

"Nay. Because it *is* the truth."

Her temper snapped. "I hate the lot of ye."

"Let us hope, it is nae always so, lass. Our marriage will be long-suffering if it is. I'd much rather we found peace with each other, even joy."

God's teeth, the man had the tongue of a sly serpent. His words flowed over her and beckoned her to accept. She gritted her teeth, unclenching them only to say, "Prepare for a long life of suffering, Broch Blackswell."

Suddenly, his fingers trailed her neck, making her shiver again. His lips brushed her ear. "I've had suffering aplenty, lass. I'd rather have pleasure with ye, as ye ken we can easily find that in each other's arms."

Before she could get her rioting emotions under control and think of a proper rejoinder, he went on. "As I was saying, upon arriving, I agreed to fight Brodee. When I took off my plaid, Blackswell saw the branding on my shoulder that he had given me as a bairn, which all firstborn Blackswell males receive from their fathers. He knew instantly I was his. He showed me his marking, exactly like mine, and then he described my mother. I dunnae recall her myself, of course, but Neil, my uncle, told me much of her."

Despite the fact that she knew asking too much and learning too many details about this man carried the danger of making her like him instead of hate him, she found herself wanting to ask more. Her heart ached for him when she considered what thinking he was a bastard for so many years had been like. She could not begrudge him the discovery that he was not, even if it did make him a Blackswell. "Did yer father tell ye why yer mother took ye and fled him?"

Broch was silent for a long moment, then he finally said, "She thought my father was still bedding the leman he'd had before he'd married my mother." Broch shrugged. "It seems my years of thinking I was a bastard were brought on by a hateful woman who told my mother that my father was still bedding her sister when it was nae true."

"That's horrid," she said, meaning it. She thought again of William's words. Was Broch honorable as William had claimed? If so, perhaps he was not seeing his family's darkness because he was simply so happy to have a true family. Maybe she could make him see them as they truly were?

"Tell me of the marking," she said, mulling upon her thoughts and what to do.

He quickly described it, and then said, "I'll show it to ye tonight in our bedchamber."

His words of not needing her heart but just her body to seal their marriage came back to her. "I will nae give myself to ye willingly!" she burst out, angry again at his words, even though she'd probably deserved them after what she had said to him.

"I'll nae force ye, lass," he said, surprising her once again. "I dunnae want ye any way but willing."

"What of the need to seal our wedding? What of the public bedding?" She had heard some of the Blackswell warriors already joking about it.

"Dunnae fash yerself."

"I'm supposed to trust ye?" she asked incredulously.

"Aye. Always," he answered so cockily that she ground her teeth. "I trusted ye nae to allow yerself to be fooled by the Blackswells. I warned ye! And tricked ye, they have!" She wanted to say more, to say that it was because he was so happy to have his own family that he could not see his own weakness, but she couldn't to bring herself to wound him so. Not tonight anyway. She would fight the battle tomorrow. With sleep and care.

Eleven

"Ye must allow us to watch ye bed her!" Brodee protested to a hearty chorus of agreement.

Even if Broch had not given his word to Katreine, which he had, he would never allow anyone to watch him bed her. He despised the tradition, and he'd never taken part in viewing it, either.

Blackswell stepped close to Broch and Katreine, who stood looking mutinous beside him. The great hall resounded with the noise of all the warriors gathered who thought to accompany him and Katreine upstairs, but even with the roar in the hall, Broch could swear he heard Katreine's labored breathing.

"Son, we are yer family now. This is our tradition."

"'Tis nae a tradition I want any part of," Broch growled.

"Ye must prove yerself worthy to be in this clan," Brodee snapped, touching a raw cord inside of Broch.

Katreine sucked in a sharp breath, and her small hand grasped his. She was deathly afraid he was going to relent, and he thought he knew why. The lass understood well the need that had long driven him to prove himself worthy to be a MacLeod. That need was still there, but he had to fight it. He understood that now, seeing that same need in Brodee to prove himself to their father. It came from within, and not simply because Broch had thought himself a bastard. Brodee had always known he was a Blackswell, and he had the same affliction as Broch, the same weakness. Broch could not give in to that itch and risk Katreine. She was his responsibility to protect.

"I dunnae need to prove myself worthy to ye or anyone," Broch said, willing himself to believe it to the marrow of his bones. "And I will leave this night and take Katreine with me back to the Isle of Skye to live with the MacLeods before I relent to a public bedding."

"Go then!" Brodee said, clearly pleased at the possibility.

"Nay!" Blackswell snapped. "Tradition be damned, then. Ye are my son, and I will nae lose ye again."

Broch felt himself relax, and he felt Katreine do so, as well. "Come," he said to his wife, leading her from the great hall as Blackswell commanded his warriors to remain there. Jeers and booing followed them into the silence of the passage, and as the great hall doors closed behind them, Katreine stopped. He turned to look at his stunning wife. "What is it?" he asked gently, awed by her beauty and strength.

"I—" She swallowed, her gaze clinging to his. The ache in his chest for her to soften to him, to ask him for his touch, shook him to the core. "Thank ye," she said simply, but it meant the world to him. "Thank ye for keeping yer word."

He wanted to touch her, to kiss her, to claim her and make her his. He wanted a life with her that he had not even realized he longed for. Yet in this moment, he would settle for her thanks. It was a beginning, however small. "I will always keep my word to ye, Katreine. I vow it to ye."

She looked on the verge of saying something else, but then she merely nodded. So he turned and walked them to their chambers. Trepidation skittered across her face as they entered the bedchamber and she looked at the bed. "I'll sleep on a pallet on the floor," he offered, wanting to ease her worry.

Glancing to the floor, she bit her lip. After a long pause, she said, "Ye may sleep in the bed with me. Just keep to yer side."

"I vow it," he said, feeling as if he had been handed a gift.

She laughed at that, then turned and presented him with her back. "Will ye unlace me?"

He'd not even considered that she would likely not wish to sleep in her gown. Desire sprang forth, throbbing through him as he slowly started to undo her bindings and, inch by inch, revealed her sheer léine and the outline of her perfect body. His hand trembled to place it upon her creamy skin, but he feared his touch would send her racing out of the room.

"I'm finished," he said, his voice a husky rumble that made him wince.

She turned swiftly toward him, her gown slipping off one shoulder to reveal the silken temptation of it, and a groan of need escaped him. Her eyes rounded, and pulling up her gown, she stepped back from him. "If ye will just turn toward the hearth," she said, her own voice husky, revealing, he suspected—and hoped—her own desire.

With a nod, he did as she asked, staring at the dancing flames of the fire. Her gown rustled and swished, and then she padded across the floor, the bed squeaked, and she said, "Ye may turn around."

When he did, it was to find her completely covered except her nose, eyes, and forehead. Her luminous eyes beckoned to him, though he knew it was not her intention, which made him grin.

"What are ye grinning at?" she demanded.

He decided instantly to be truthful. "With naught but yer wee forehead, eyes, and nose poking out of the blankets, ye are still the most alluring lass I've ever beheld."

"Are ye trying to seduce me?" she asked, her gaze narrowing.

"Most assuredly," he said with a wink. "Is it working?"

"Of course nae," she replied primly, though he could see she was fighting a smile.

An idea suddenly occurred to him of how he might actually get his willful wife to engage in a game of seduction with him. "I must try harder, then," he said.

"Och! Dunnae bother. It dunnae matter how hard ye try, ye kinnae seduce me."

"Nay?" He cocked his eyebrows.

"Nay," she said smugly.

"Do ye care to wager?"

She frowned. "What sort of wager?"

He thought of earlier when she had unknowingly grabbed his hand for reassurance in the great hall, and an idea came to him. "Every time ye touch me, I get one kiss."

"Bah!" She waved a hand at him. "I will easily nae ever touch ye. What sort of wager is that? I dunnae win anything."

"Ye win the satisfaction of kenning ye bested me."

"'Tis nae enough," she announced like a true shrewd bargainer. "If I have nae touched ye in a sennight, ye will spend the next sennight with me questioning yer clan about the raids upon my family. And then we will discover the truth."

"'Tis a bargain," he agreed, swallowing the triumphant grin of his victory.

Katreine awoke slowly, feeling cozy and groggy and not wishing to open her eyes. In fact, she wished to go back to sleep and recapture the dream she'd been having. She couldn't remember the specifics, but she'd been happy in the dream.

"Ye're touching me, lass," came Broch's voice, so near that his warm breath fanned her cheek. Her eyes flew open, and she gasped. She lay face-to-face with Broch, their noses nearly touching. His piercing blue eyes were locked upon her. He had a smug smile on his lips, and she realized, to her horror, she was indeed touching him. She had her leg draped over his and her arm around his waist.

She jerked her arm and her leg back to the sound of his chuckle.

"I'll take my kiss now." His tone was uncompromising but oddly gentle.

She did not like the way her heart stuttered in anticipation. This wager had been a bad idea. "It dunnae signify if I'm sleeping."

"Tsk, tsk, Katreine. I did nae take ye for the sort of lass to nae keep a promise."

He gave her a knowing look for one bated breath, and she was sure he must have known of the vow she had made to her father. But that was impossible. She stared at her too-handsome husband and a keen wish to discover whether he was as honorable as she'd thought previously or a deceptive Blackswell at heart strummed through her. And then what? What would she do with what she learned? Even if he was a good and honorable man, that certainly did not mean his family was of the same nature. She could never live with them or simply dismiss what they had done.

Suddenly, Broch's fingers trailed light as a feather down her cheek and his desirous expression stilled her. "Forget what it is ye're agonizing over for just one kiss, lass. I vow one kiss will nae decide yer fate."

The man could persuade a warrior to set down his sword in the middle of battle, he was that forceful. Despite knowing this, she still found herself nodding and saying, "I stand by my vows."

His large hands took her face and cupped it, and it felt as if her entire body filled with wanting for this man. His gaze became as soft as a caress. "I hope nae," he said, and her mouth parted with the shock that he *did* know of her promise to her father. But before she could respond, he captured her mouth with his. His hands left her face and circled her waist, dragging her toward him in a hard embrace as his lips went from tantalizingly light, persuasive kissing to fiery possession.

Shock waves roiled through her at not only the hunger and need of his kiss but of the way her body was responding to him. Yearning pulsed deep within her at her core, and her breasts became heavy and aching. Her heart beat too fast, and her blood rushed through her veins as if it could not move quickly enough from her heart to the rest of her body.

His tongue twined with hers, and a moan escaped her as his hard staff pressed into her stomach. She could not seem to stop her reaction to him. She pushed her pelvis against him, asking him to touch her without saying the words. His fingers slid from her waist to between her legs, tracing the sensitive skin with such gentleness that she wanted to weep from the pleasure and scream with the need he was invoking.

When his fingers went to the part of her that throbbed

the most, she grasped his shoulder, digging her nails deep into his skin. Her mind was a loud whir of breath, and heartbeats, and rushing blood. She could not think beyond the slide of his hands down her thighs as he removed her underclothing and the way his strong fingers parted her core with such gentleness.

She cried out when he touched a place on her she had not known existed, and then he seemed to know exactly what to do. He moved with the precision of an expert hunter, stalking her with little circles that made her need grow to a frenzy until she thrashed her head back and forth, needing some sort of release. "Please!" she begged.

Without a word, he gave her what she had not known she needed. His fingers became as frenzied as her yearning, making everything within her coil and feel taut to the point of breaking, and then she did break. She shattered into a thousand blissful pieces as wave after wave of warmth and pleasure poured through her and unwound the coil Broch had created.

His powerful body came between her legs, his thighs spreading hers, and she was certain then that he was going to seal their marriage as she knew he wanted to, needed to. And she felt she did not have the strength nor the desire to stop him. She wanted him. It was treacherous: she wanted a man who was the son of her enemy, brother of the murderer of her sister.

The smile that had been on Broch's lips faded to a sardonic twist of his mouth. "Ye dunnae have to hate me," he said. It was a statement, but she also heard the pleading in his voice.

A tear slipped from her eye, which shocked her. She started to wipe it away, but Broch's fingers were there before she could even move. "Tell me what I can do."

"I wish I kenned," she replied honestly. "Even if I find ye honorable, ye are still a Blackswell. I kinnae forgive yer family or live in peace among them."

He nodded, appearing to think upon what she had said. "Let us first see if ye find me honorable, aye? 'Tis a place to start."

She should say no, but what she should do never seemed to reconcile with what she actually did when it came to this man, so she nodded. But even as she did, she vowed to herself that there would be no more kisses. She could not touch Broch again because, clearly, she had no control where he was concerned.

Twelve

His wife had a will that would put many a warrior to shame. Three days. It had been three days since she had touched him. He had been impressed and irked with the clever way she had fixed her problem of stopping herself from becoming entangled with him when she slept. Several rolled-up blankets now divided their bed into two sections, one for him and for her. He despised it. Yet he could not help but be proud of how she endeavored to stick to the promise she had given her father, however misguided it was.

In the last few days, he had striven to show her the good that he had come to see in the Blackswell clan, but obviously it was not enough. He had taken her to cook in the kitchens with the friendly women one day, and though Katreine had begrudgingly admitted they were nice and seemed honest enough, she had also said the men were the problem, not the women.

So the next day he'd had her talk to Father Donnely, who Broch had spoken with himself two sennights before when making his own inquiries about the clan. She'd asked the white-haired, gray-bearded, gentle-eyed man if he suspected anyone in the clan would be going to Hell for murder and theft.

Broch had been forced to clench his teeth on a chuckle

at her indirect yet direct question and Father Donnely's shocked expression. The priest had stammered about and then told Katreine that he believed all the Blackswells to be in good standing with God, to which she had patted the portly priest's hand and said in a placating tone that she understood he had to say that. She'd not stopped there though, no. She'd said that she was certain God would forgive Father Donnely for his falsehood begotten by fear of punishment. Father Donnely had turned red as a beet and tried to say a prayer for her, but instead, she'd taken out a coin to pay for a penance for him.

On the third day, Broch had woken with such a sharp ache to touch his new wife, to kiss her, that he'd been bound and determined that this would be the day she saw some good in the family they were both now tied to. He'd taken her to speak with the bard, Alban, who knew the history of the clan. The man had told them that the Blackswell healer Esmerelda had birthed Broch and Brodee, and then he'd told tales of the Blackswells' daring feats for King David and his father. The bard had spoken of the honor of Broch's father and the ferociousness of Brodee in battle, which had won King David his last victory in the Rough Bounds. Unfortunately, Katreine had seen that same ferociousness as the very thing that pointed to Brodee being a murderer.

Now, morning had come again, and Broch was at a loss as to what to do next. He sat in the great hall alone, as most people had not even risen yet. He stared at the rich tapestries hanging on the walls, which depicted battle scenes the Blackswells had been engaged in over the years, and he wondered if there would ever be a tapestry made depicting him with his father and brother. It was the first time he had allowed himself to think of the Blackswell as his actual father. He'd hesitated to do so, he supposed because he was being careful, wanting to ensure he did not actually uncover something he had missed that would show the man as guilty of the things Katreine was convinced he—and Brodee—had done. As far as Broch could see, the only thing that Blackswell was guilty of was his harshness toward Brodee.

Broch desperately wanted to carve a place for himself in this clan, but how could he do that when his wife hated his family? He drummed his fingers on the table trying to order his thoughts when footsteps fell in the great hall, and he turned to see his father striding toward him.

"Why do ye look so vexed?" Blackswell asked, sitting down beside Broch.

"I kinnae unravel how to make Katreine see that Brodee is innocent of murdering her sister…" He eyed his father, knowing the man had previously worried Brodee may have done it.

Blackswell shook his head. "Yer brother is nae a murderer. That was foolish of me. Brodee has nae ever raised a hand to harm a lass. Truth be told, he loved his leman and wished to wed her, but I told him he could nae. I told him that he had to wed Lenora so we could obtain half of Derthshire. I shamed him, I'm sorry to say. I made him feel he'd ruined so many things. I even said I would nae be surprised if he somehow ruined our chance at obtaining the land."

"Ye are too hard on him," Broch said, deciding it was finally time to speak his mind.

"Aye. I did nae ever realize how cold and distant I've been to him until ye came back into my life, Son. Ye returned a warmth to me that I suppose I'd denied myself out of guilt for kenning I drove yer mother away."

Broch nodded. "I suspected the guilt part." He didn't know what to say about the warmth part. He was not a man for soft conversation or words. Still, he cleared his throat. "I, er, feel glad to have found ye, as well."

Blackswell grinned at that, which was a great relief. Broch would rather yank out a tooth than sit and exchange soft words with his father. Blackswell clapped Broch on the shoulder. "Give yer new wife some time. Why dunnae ye focus on finding yer place in the clan? Once ye have, she will see and follow."

Broch nodded. "Perhaps. My current plot is nae working."

Blackswell chuckled. "Well, I'd like to give ye the training of my personal guards. I'm too old to be doing this anymore."

"I'll take it," Broch said, thinking about Brodee. "But only if ye give me half the responsibility. Give Brodee half, as well, aye?"

Blackswell nodded, his eyes shining with what Broch swore was pride. "Ye are going to make a fine laird someday."

And damned if the praise did not lodge a lump in Broch's throat.

Katreine hid behind a crowd of women who had gathered to watch the afternoon training of Blackswell's personal guards, and she scowled. She stared at her husband, clad only in his braies, which clung sinfully to his hips, and her stomach tightened. She knew the feeling well. He laughed with the men, even his brother for a moment, which made her clench her teeth so hard that a pain shot through her jaw.

For a sennight now, Broch had spent all his mornings and days training with these men, including Brodee. At first, she'd been ecstatic when she'd learned he and his brother were to train the personal guard together, because she'd been certain that would give Broch a chance to see that his brother was evil. But Brodee was apparently cleverer than she had thought.

They had disagreed at first, and Brodee still seemed very reluctant to share control with Broch, but to her dismay, he seemed to be gaining Broch's allegiance. At supper the last several nights, they'd sat laughing about training stories from the day, and the two of them had taken to swimming in the loch after supper and staying out so late that she'd been asleep the last three nights when Broch had come to their bedchamber.

Things could not continue this way. She had to somehow show Broch what his family was really like, and…and…what? Frustration made her curl her hands into fists, even as her gaze was riveted to Broch, who launched an attack on Brodee to show the other warriors defense moves.

Broch moved with the grace of a God and the skill of a man born to conquer. He made her mouth water and her thoughts spin. God's teeth! She lusted for her husband! Not only that but, to her dismay, she liked him. Tremendously. She might even be starting to care for him. Perhaps, if she could somehow make him see the treachery that surrounded him, he would come with her to her home. There, they could live together, learn each other, and—she swallowed as a newfound hope welled in her—they could even love each other.

She watched as Broch spun out of a blow Brodee had

sent toward him, then circled behind his brother, relieved him of his sword, and knocked him to the ground. The crowd cheered for Broch as he held out his hand to Brodee to help him off the ground, but as he did, one of the men called out, "We see who the best warrior is!" In that instant, the laughter that had been on Brodee's face vanished, he smacked Broch's hand away, and bounding to his feet, stomped off.

Though it appeared the man was on the verge of showing his true self, Katreine did not feel triumph. Hurt flickered across Broch's features for a moment before a blank expression replaced it. He turned when another warrior asked him something, and within seconds, he was training again.

Behind her, a voice said, "They will find their way. Ye will see."

She turned, recognizing Blackswell's voice. "What I saw is yer youngest son about to reveal who he really is."

"Nay, lass," Blackswell said. "What ye saw is Brodee hurt by words because of injuries and insecurities I myself gave him. For that, I'm guilty."

She flinched at his words. He knew she was searching for guilt in their clan. "We shall see," she snapped and started to turn from him, but he gently took hold of her wrist. With a glance over her shoulder, she said, "What?"

"Have ye considered what would happen if ye manage to convince Broch of what ye believe and then discover later that ye are wrong? How do ye think he would feel discovering ye robbed him of more time with the family that was lost to him for so long?"

"I'm nae wrong," she growled, snatching her wrist away and storming from the courtyard. She didn't know where she was going, but when she found herself at the top of the cliffs and she glanced down, she bit her lip, realizing she had unconsciously gone to the place where she believed her sister had been pushed. Katreine looked to where Lenora's body had been found. She stared until the rock became blurry, her mind turning, doubting, questioning. What if she *was* wrong? What if she convinced Broch of what she believed, but then discovered she was not right, as Blackswell said? Broch would likely never forgive her.

"I did nae kill her."

With a gasp, she turned around and found Brodee standing there. Her heart began to race. "Did ye follow me?" she asked, looking beyond him to the pebbled path that led to where she stood.

"Nay. I came here after I fought Broch. I come here often."

"Out of guilt!" she challenged.

He scowled at her. "Aye. But not because I murdered yer sister." He stepped toward her, and she instinctually scuttled back, looking behind her to ensure she'd not fall. She had no room left to step away again. She sucked in a breath to try to calm her thundering heart. "If ye did nae kill her, why do ye feel guilty?"

"I feel accountable for her death, ye see. I did nae kill Arabel, my leman, either. And my own da did nae believe me!"

She didn't know if that was desperation or anguish in his tone, but it frightened her. She scanned her surroundings, thinking she had just enough room to dodge between him and the trees to escape him. She edged a bit to the left, relieved when he didn't move. Maybe she could lead him to say something to reveal the truth.

"That is nae a thing to feel guilt for," she said. "Be truthful."

"I saw her. I saw yer sister the night she was killed."

"I kenned it!" Katreine gasped. "Ye did murder her!"

"Nay!" He stepped in front of her, blocking the path she had so foolishly not taken. Sweat instantly dampened her brow, and her pulse exploded. He held his palms up as if he sensed her fear. "I came here when she sent a note asking me to, and I answered her questions about Arabel. I was truthful. I told her that I had loved Arabel and wanted to wed her, but my father made me end it to wed yer sister. I would nae ever have harmed Arabel, nor yer sister. I left her here crying but alive, and for that, I will forever hold guilt and shame in my heart. I dunnae den who killed yer sister, but it was nae me."

"Ye expect me to believe ye after ye just admitted ye lied?" she demanded, her fright racing with her thoughts of her sister, her mother in grief, her own grief, her father's and brothers' hatred of Brodee and all Blackswells.

"Listen to me," he pleaded.

"Nay!" she cried out, feeling enormous guilt herself because there was a part of her that did want to listen. If Brodee was innocent of murder, her future with Broch would be so much easier, even if the Blackswells were guilty of the raids. "I will nae hear more. Leave me be."

For a moment, dread filled her that he wouldn't. He raised his hand, and she was terrified for one breath that he would shove her. His shoulders sagged, and he looked almost stricken. The man was so good at showing a false face. Then he turned without a word and went down the pebbled path to the right, instead of the one she'd taken here on the left.

She faced the cliff once more and wrapped her arms around herself as the wind blew her hair back and wafted a cool breeze over her, raising gooseflesh on her arms. He'd sounded so earnest and looked so hurt that she stood there battered by the noise of doubt in her mind. A crunch behind her, footfalls on the pebbles, cut through her thoughts, but before she could turn, she was violently shoved, getting out no more than a scream before she tumbled off the ledge toward the cliffs below.

Thirteen

About halfway down the trail to the cliffs where Broch suspected Katreine had gone when she'd left the courtyard, a woman's scream filled the silence. A wave of icy fear swept through him as he raced down the remainder of the narrow, twisting, pebbled path, shoving branches out of the way as he ran. Just as he came to the opening that led to a small clearing, he saw Brodee standing there, looking down toward the rocks below, and rage tore through him as anguish stabbed his heart.

He'd been wrong to trust Brodee.

The single thought rang in his head as he raced to close the distance to the ledge that overlooked the cliffs. As Broch ran toward his brother, he registered him dropping to the ground on his stomach, and then yelling, "Take my hand!"

Overwhelming relief that Katreine had to still be alive made him stumble. His hand grazed the ground and he gained steady footing once more. He reached his brother, whose fingers were now interlocked with Katreine's. The terrified look on Katreine's face felt like a dagger to his gut.

"Dunnae fash yerself, lass." He tried to make his voice calm, even as his gaze slid the long distance down to the rocks below where she would surely meet her death if she fell.

"I have ye," Brodee vowed as he began to try to pull her

up, but the rock that had stopped her from falling all the way to her death was also now making it difficult to bring her up. It jutted out sharply, and she needed to be pulled over it.

"Ye pushed me!" Katreine hissed.

"Nay," Brodee cried, even as he worked to bring her over the rock to which she clung.

Broch could see the muscles of Brodee's arms straining. Sweat trickled down his brother's face, and his cheeks were deep red with his effort. He feared his brother was not going to be able to keep his hold on Katreine. He quickly assessed the situation. Brodee had his body braced with his feet and his left palm, while his right hand held on to Katreine's right hand.

Broch reached his left hand down to his wife, their eyes locking. "Take my hand, lass," he encouraged her. She nodded, released the rock she'd had a death grip on, and swung her arm toward his.

She screamed when her body rocked and Brodee swayed, and Broch's heart felt as if it were plummeting to the rocks below. He stretched out, catching the sleeve of her gown, then her arm, which he wrapped his hand around. Just as he did, her hand slipped from Brodee's and the weight of her body sent Broch into a sudden slide toward the ledge. He grasped at the dirt and the pebbles with his free hand, finally stopping the momentum pulling him toward death.

His heart thundered, not for himself but Katreine. Her face was white, and her lips pressed thin. As he tightened his grip, Brodee grasped his legs. "I'll hold ye, Brother!"

Broch nodded, keeping his gaze on Katreine's. She'd not uttered another sound to indicate her fright, but it shone brightly in her eyes. "I will nae let go," he vowed to her.

"Dunnae ye let go, either, damn ye. Dunnae ye dare leave me."

Her eyes grew wide at that. "I'll nae release ye, either," she promised him.

He had a feeling they were both speaking of more than this moment. He began to pull her up over the rock, and within a few breaths, she was close enough that he leaned farther over and grasped both her arms to give her a sharp tug up over the final ledge.

He brought her body to his, wrapped his arms around her, and rolled her on top of him as he lay on the hard surface, panting, his wife in his arms. She had smudges of dirt on her face, and her hair was a wild, tangled mess. "Ye look even more beautiful than the first moment I saw ye," he blurted.

Her rosy lips parted, showing her surprise. "Yer eyesight must be horrid, then," she said, smiling.

"'Tis perfect," he assured her. He could not make himself let her go yet, and she did not seem to want him to do so. She clung to him, her eyes warm and inviting, so he held her tightly, her body pressed to his, their hearts thundering in time, and their breath mingling each time one of them exhaled. He had to win this lass, for she had already captured a part of him without him knowing it.

Brodee cleared his throat beside them, and Broch looked to his brother. "I did nae push ye," Brodee said, his voice emphatic.

"I dunnae believe ye," Katreine snapped, the warmth leaving her eyes as she pushed off Broch and stood. She pointed a shaky finger at Brodee. "Who else would have done it? Ye were here moments before I fell, and ye were here after I fell."

Broch stood and studied Brodee, looking for signs of

guilt or innocence. Brodee's face appeared open and his eyes true. "Why the devil would I try to save ye if I had pushed ye?" Brodee demanded.

"Because ye kenned yer brother saw ye!" Katreine bellowed.

But he'd not seen Brodee push her. Broch stared at Brodee, and he did not see guilt. Maybe that made him a fool, but his gut told him Brodee was innocent. "I did nae see him push ye," Broch said, to which Brodee gave him a grateful look, and Katreine shot him a frustrated one.

"Ye're blinded by yer desire to have a family," she accused.

"I dunnae believe so, lass," he said gently, not wishing to fight with his wife, whom he'd almost lost. "I saw him try to save ye."

"Then answer me this," she demanded, not sounding at all convinced, "if yer brother did nae push me, nor kill my sister, then who did?"

He exchanged a long look with Brodee. His brother didn't know, and neither did he, but he intended to find out. "I dunnae ken," he admitted, to which Katreine threw up her hands before brushing past them, limping and cursing. Broch frowned, hating that his wife was hurt.

"I appreciate yer belief in me," Brodee said. "I'm sorry I've nae been more welcoming."

Broch nodded. He knew why his brother had acted as he had: Brodee was jealous of their father's reception of him. Broch could not say he would have acted differently if he'd been treated the way Brodee had by their father. "I intend to find the person who tried to kill my wife."

"I intend to help ye," Brodee responded with a hard look.

Broch inclined his head in thanks. "I'll see her to the

safety of our chamber and then meet ye back here."

"I can scout this area, if ye want to stay with her for a bit. I believe yer wife may be shaken up, though she appears too stubborn to ever admit it."

Broch chuckled. "I believe ye are correct, but I'll nae be able to rest until we have scoured the cliffs. I'll just ensure she makes the chamber, and then I'll return. Take a care, aye?"

Brodee nodded. "Aye. Ye too."

As Broch turned to go after Katreine, Brodee spoke once more. "I had thought at first that whoever killed Arabel and then Lenora must hate me, but after this incident, I think mayhap they hate all Blackswells."

Broch thought about that for a moment. "Have there been more killings, or attempted killings, in the clan in the years since that ye can recall?"

"Nay," Brodee answered immediately, "which means my new thinking was nae correct."

"I believe," Broch said, considering, "that whoever killed yer leman and Katreine's sister, and tried to kill Katreine, dunnae hate *all* Blackswells."

Brodee nodded. "They hate us," he said, motioning between the two of them.

"Aye," Broch replied. "They hate the heirs of Blackswell."

The question was, why?

※

Katreine paced the small confines of her bedchamber, cutting through the shadows brought on by the night as she muttered. *Stay here,* he'd demanded. He'd return shortly, he'd said. That had been hours ago! She marched to the window that overlooked the courtyard and cursed at the empty space. Why was she obeying her husband anyway?

She drummed her fingers on the window ledge as the question repeated in her mind. Why? Why was she listening to a Blackswell?

I will nae let go… Dunnae ye dare leave me.

His words echoed straight to her heart, making it beat faster. That was why she was still here. She could not ignore that plea. In truth, she did not want to. Broch had a claim on her whether she wished it or not, and she was not entirely certain that she did not wish it. He had shown her nothing but honor, and caring, and need. A need she also felt and wanted to fulfill with him.

She continued to pace their bedchamber as she thought. The man was blind when it came to his family, and she could not seem to make him see the truth. His brother had pushed her. The only reason Brodee had tried to save her was because he'd known Broch would kill him if he suspected that Brodee had done so. She had to smile at that. Her husband was protective of her, and for once in her life, she did not mind it in the least. It was nice to know someone was always watching out for her. She intended to do the same for him.

She needed a different plan, and thinking upon his words, she decided that it was time for them to officially seal their marriage. She had to admit she was eager for it, and if Broch was half as eager as she was, which she suspected he was, then his desire not to lose her would be so complete that he'd surely agree to go live with her clan and not stay here among liars and killers.

Just as her decision was made, the door to their bedchamber opened with a swish, and her compelling husband stepped over the threshold, making her breath hitch, her belly tighten, and a thrill course through her. The wary look he gave her almost made her chuckle. He expected a battle, and she was launching one, it was true, but secretly and disguised under sweet surrender.

He shut the door behind him, then stopped as if uncertain what to say or do. She was glad to see her husband had uncertainties, too. "Did ye discover anything?" she asked.

He shook his head, and she pressed her lips together on telling him that he'd not found anything because the person responsible had been looking with him. When he arched his eyebrows at her, she swallowed a laugh. He was surprised she had not launched into blaming his brother. Good. Maybe her new line of attack would work.

"I dunnae wish to quarrel," she said, taking heart when he smiled with obvious relief.

"Neither do I, lass." He walked toward her and reached out, then stilled. And she thought she knew why. She captured his searing gaze as she pressed her palm to his heart. Underneath her fingertips, his warmth seeped into her and the steady beat of his life comforted her.

He smiled slowly, devilishly. "Ye're touching me."

She nodded, licking her lips in anticipation of what she hoped was about to happen.

His brows dipped together in bafflement. "Ye recall that touching me means I get to claim a kiss?"

"Aye," she said, purposely rubbing her fingers back and forth over the hard muscle of his chest.

"What are ye doing, lass?" His tone sounded strained, as if he were struggling to control something. She very much hoped it was his desire for her.

"I'm attempting to get ye to seal our wedding vows without asking ye."

He caught her fingers, pressed them to his lips, and then

released them as his other hand slid to the small of her back. A triumphant gleam came to his eyes.

Good. Let him think he had won.

"Nae that I'm nae verra pleased to hear this, *mo bhean mhaiseach,* but I am surprised. Why the change?" he asked.

The strong emotion that gripped her when he called her *my beautiful wife* scared her a little. What if she could not persuade him to come with her? What if all she accomplished was him sending her away and never coming for her? The thought made her breath hitch deep within, but she had to press on. She didn't see another way.

She reached up and grasped his plaid, then started to unwrap it as her blood sang in heady anticipation. "I almost died, and ye risked yer life to save me."

She let the plaid drop to the floor between them, and she raked her gaze boldly over Broch's perfect form. She wanted to run her fingers over the dips and swells, the muscle and bone of what made him such a man.

He slipped his hands into her hair, his fingers sliding over her scalp and making her hiss before he cradled her neck with his strong hands. "I've risked my life to save ye before," he said, his gaze seeming to delve into her. She had the feeling he was sifting through her eyes to try to discover her secrets. "Tell me the truth," he demanded. "Why are ye standing before me now, giving yerself to me this night?"

Because ye've already claimed me in heart and spirit.

The thought shocked her. She could not say that. She would not reveal such a weakness, but she would not outright lie. "I'm waging a battle," she replied, running her hands over his chest and low to his abdomen. His muscles twitched under her touch, and he groaned.

His hands moved from her neck to round over her shoulders, then took a sinful path to her breasts, which he grazed first with his palms and then his fingers. The same heavy ache as before filled her, and the tight, pulsing need deep at her core sprang forth just as the night he had touched her after they were wed. "A war, ye say?" he asked in a husky growl.

She had trouble pulling her thoughts from the sensations his fingers sparked as they swept back and forth over her buds. When he lightly pinched her sensitive nipples, she gasped and leaned toward him. "Aye," she said, her voice breaking with her rapidly mounting yearning.

"Have ye nae heard I'm a legendary warrior?" he asked, capturing her mouth in a burning, ravenous kiss before she could answer.

He swept his tongue into her mouth like a man bent on victory. In this, she would gladly surrender. She met his kiss with her own wild need, gliding her hands down between them and tentatively touching his hardness. She'd never done such a thing, but when he growled and his kiss became harder and faster, she felt quite certain he wanted more of her touch.

She traced her finger over the long line of his staff, which she could feel under the material of his braies. He broke away from her mouth, kissing a path down her neck and then sliding his tongue over her collarbone before his fingers worked with shocking expertise and quickness to relieve her of her gown and undergarments. When the last bit of her clothing fell away and the cool air chilled her skin, shyness suddenly hit her with the realization that she stood completely bare in front of him. She went to cross her arms over her chest, but he moved so quickly she'd not even realized he had, until he caught both of her wrists in a firm hold. Slowly, he opened her arms wide, his grip on her wrists tightening ever so slightly.

"Exquisite." His voice was deep and rich as it washed over her. Her cheeks heated under his gaze, which moved over her like a caress before returning to her face. "Ye are so verra beautiful, Katreine," he murmured. "Dunnae ever feel ye need to hide from me. Ye are so lovely on the outside it makes me ache, but ye are as lovely on the inside. And that, that beauty is the truest ever."

"Oh, the lasses that must have tumbled at yer feet before me," she said, feeling even more vulnerable because his words spoke to her heart and to the part of her that always had hoped to find love.

He placed his large palm over her heart as she had done to his earlier. "I have nae ever spoken words like the ones I just did to ye, lass. This I vow upon my honor."

That vow nearly undid her. She wanted to fling herself into his arms. Instead, she said, "Shush now, Husband, and show me how a legendary warrior attempts to conquer a woman."

He grinned then, looking very much like a fox who'd snagged his prey, and in the space of a breath, she was in his arms, and he'd carried her to the bed and carefully laid her upon it. He managed to rid himself of his braies as he came to hover above her, the bed creaking under his added weight. She caught her breath in anticipation of kissing him again, but he surprised her when he took her ankle and lifted her leg.

He traced his fingers over the slope of her calf before his lips followed the same path. Her blood rushed through her veins, fast and furious and deep within her. The need only he had ever stirred screamed to be sated. "Broch," she said, as desperation to know the feeling of him inside her nipped at her patience.

He glanced at her and gave her a taunting smile. "Patience, my Valkyrie."

Her eyes widened. Never had she told anyone that she fancied herself a descendant of the fierce women of old Viking legends.

He lowered her leg back to the bed, and even the soft blanket was almost painful on the flesh made so sensitive from his lips. Then his hands pressed between her thighs, and he spread them wide, making her blush once more.

"Perfection here, as well," he rasped, the top of his head disappearing from her view as he kissed first her inner right thigh and then the left. Her core tightened, making her feel taut as a bow about to be released. "I want to taste ye." He parted her at her core, shocking her, and before she could fully register what he'd done, his tongue slid slowly, tantalizingly across her flesh. The sensations that came next were so strong, so powerful, that she arched upward and let out a moan. She delved her hands into his hair to ensure he would not leave her just yet.

He chuckled, sounding surely just like the Devil when he knew a poor individual had lost the will to fight their desires. Broch's tongue found the spot that throbbed, and he circled it, lavished it, and suckled it until she could not hold back the ecstasy that claimed her and melted her like steel to be molded in his strong hands.

As waves of pleasure rippled over her, Broch rose, slid his hands under her bottom, and thrust into her so powerfully that she was certain he had splintered her. A cry was on her lips, but he smothered it with a searing kiss. He began to move within her, and her body stretched to accommodate him as she grew used to him. Within a few heartbeats, the pain had disappeared. She could not think beyond the need to learn his rhythm and match him, and soon they were moving as one to a place she knew would be even better than moments ago.

The tension inside her began to build again, quickly like a storm that claimed the sky so suddenly one had no time to take shelter. Broch was that storm, and he was battering down upon her soul, claiming it and making her his. She clung to his powerful arms as the tide of ecstasy lifted her up and tossed her about. And then, as she fell toward luxurious oblivion, Broch cried out, tensed, and joined her in the freefall to utter bliss.

When they both began to catch their breath, he rolled off her, but his fingers caught hers, threading them together. She turned her head to steal a glance at his profile but found him staring at her as if committing her to memory. A new ache sprang up in her chest, and she suspected she knew what it was. She had fallen in love with her husband, and that was a weakness, to be certain, for the battle to come.

Fourteen

Broch could watch Katreine sleep for hours. In rest, the lines of determination that had been ever-present between her brows since accompanying him to the Blackswell keep would smooth. She looked so peaceful. She took long, deep, slow breaths and had a smile upon her face, which he liked to think he had something to do with. Every once in a while, she would murmur something, and he wondered if her dreaming mind was going over her strategy to persuade him to leave Hightower. His instinct had kept him alive in more battles than he could even recall, and he had no doubt that was what she was planning to do. She had the mind of a fighter, his lass.

At first, he had been confused when he entered the bedchamber and she did not immediately start to argue about Brodee. But then when she'd begun her seduction he'd known. He was pleased she'd not lied about it, and he was impressed with the clever way she had avoided doing so. She had said simply that she was waging a battle without admitting anything specific. Whether she intended it as a hint on how to prepare or not, he couldn't be sure.

As she slept, he pondered what she might be plotting. In her mind, she was in danger and they were living among liars and murderers. He frowned. Unfortunately, she was not entirely wrong on the murderer account. Someone had pushed her, and someone had killed Brodee's leman and Katreine's sister years before. Who and why were the questions he needed answered, and it would be far easier to focus on discovering the truth with Katreine returned to the safety of her own home. As much as he hated the thought of parting with her, until he knew who was trying to kill his wife, it was best to take her where she would be well away from danger.

And yet, as much as he knew she wanted to return to Thioram, he thought perhaps if he commanded it, she would resist, and if he forced it, she might do something impulsive and stubborn, such as leaving for Thioram on her own. And deep within him, in the part that understood his wife had a grip on his heart now, he hoped she would not wish to depart without him, that this night, with the act they had just shared, they had sealed their marriage vows in a way no man could ever destroy.

With that in mind, he decided that he would see what her plan of attack was and then revise his own to best her for her own good. Feeling content with his choice, he turned onto his side to get a better view of Katreine as she slept. Moonlight streamed through the window, making her look like an angel. His angel, whom he'd die to protect.

Long ago he'd given up believing he would ever truly feel like part of a family, and now here he was, lying beside his wife in his father's castle. It almost scared him that all he had ever wanted was here before him. He could not allow himself to be content and relaxed—not yet. That's when the enemy always struck.

"Ye're wrong about Brodee," the muleheaded man said

once again, just as he had for the last hour. They'd been arguing since waking, much to Katreine's frustration, and the desire to shake sense into her husband nearly overwhelmed her. But it would do no good to even try. For one thing, he was much larger and stronger than she was, and for another, it was clear his mind was made up and was as unchangeable as the surety that moments slipped through one's fingers no matter how tight one held them.

"Fine," she said, not relenting but trying a different approach. "Let me prove to ye that ye are wrong. Let us seek the truth together."

"Nay," he said, his tone unyielding.

"But—"

"Nay."

The word rang with a finality that made her want to throttle him. Broch was leaving her no choice. He would not see the truth of his family, and he would not let her show him the truth by seeking it. The only option she had left was extreme: she was going to have to make him want to send her back to her home and hope that he'd miss her so much that he'd relent to either coming to live with her at Thioram or to search out the truth of his brother and his clan.

She inhaled a deep fortifying breath. She didn't like it, but she was going to have to hurt him in order to protect him from his family. "Ye're a fool. Ye're so eager to carve a place in yer newfound family that ye are blind! I'd rather nae have a husband than have one who is a Blackswell," she flung out.

Broch narrowed his eyes upon her. "Careful, lass. Nae having a husband around can be arranged if ye push me."

"Fine," she bit out, hating what she was doing but pleased her plan was starting out so well. At this rate, he'd likely wish to return her to her father in a sennight. No, she smiled inwardly. It would probably take a fortnight to get him to despise her. "Tell me how hard to shove and I will."

"Oh, ye'll ken when I've reached my limit of what I'm willing to swallow," he thundered, then turned on his heel and stormed from the room.

She frowned a little as she watched him depart, and a feeling of vulnerability invaded her again. She'd fallen in love with her husband, but what if he did not hold the same feelings for her? Her plan could be her ruin, and—She forced the foolish thought away. Her plan would be their salvation!

She launched her plan later that morning after discovering her husband was in the clearing training his men. If he was anything like her brothers and father, he would despise that she was interrupting his training, so she trotted down to the site, almost laughing to herself at the numerous trivial things she had thought of as reasons for her interruption.

He was in the midst of a full combat sequence when she shoved through the warriors circling her husband and his brother, and cleared her throat. Concentrated as both men were, neither of them saw her draw close, though several of Broch's warriors did call out for her to halt. She intended to tap Broch on the shoulder, but then he reared back his elbow. She gasped and ducked, almost getting slammed in the nose.

He swung around, his jaw going slack before a dark look settled on his face. "What the devil are ye doing, lass?"

She smiled and purposely batted her eyelashes, hoping she looked like a vacuous fool. She held up a green ribbon and a blue one. "Which color should I wear in my hair for supper?"

"Ye risked yerself by coming near me during training to ask about ribbon?" Incredulity saturated his tone.

"Aye," she said sweetly. "I have a horrid time making choices. I always have. My brothers and my father learned over the years just to answer my questions. Otherwise, I really can get quite vexed."

"I dunnae give a care what ribbon ye wear," he snapped. "But I do care that ye interrupted my training. Dunnae do it again unless it is life or death, aye? Especially, dunnae put yerself in peril. I mean that, Katreine," he added, his expression tight.

His response was perfect and made her want to kiss him. He cared for her. He wanted to protect her. It would take some doing to get him to send her away, but once he did and missed her, he would come for her, and then he would be more reasonable.

Broch pressed his mouth close to her ear. "If ye're injured by yer own foolishness, it will reflect badly on me that I kinnae protect my own wife, even though it would be yer fault." He withdrew and gave her an expectant, impatient look that surprised her.

"Oh," was all she managed to utter, because her throat felt as if it was closing. Surely, that was not what he truly cared about? No, no, he was simply irritated. She swallowed and said in a tone she hoped was terse and not worrisome, "I'll do my best nae to get foolishly injured." She turned to stride away, but her steps faltered at five paces, ten, fifteen, then twenty. Was he not going to call her back? She had been sure he would.

She would not glance back at him. She would not. She took five more steps before she gave into her burning desire to peek over her shoulder. He wasn't even paying any mind to her departure! He was already training his men once more. Her chest squeezed as she turned around and kept walking. By the time she made her way to the kitchens, she felt horrible and sad, and completely unsure of herself.

She half-listened as she was directed by the head of the kitchen on what she could do to aid them. Her mind replayed Broch's words to her over and over, as well as his seeming lack of caring. Likely, he'd just been angry. Worry invaded her. What if it was that he did not care for her, and here she was, trying to get him to send her away? No, she was being foolish. He cared, and she would continue her strategy.

With this in mind, she put all her effort into kneading the dough for the bread. When she caught several women frowning at her, she realized that she was practically beating the dough. Biting her lip, she took a calming breath and forced herself to calm down, and then she continued her task until the sun was high in the sky signaling midday, and she took a break to seek out Broch once more.

He was still training, but this time he was working with his warriors on archery. They were in the clearing once more, and she started down the hill only to trip on a rock, lose her footing, and go rolling down the slope. She landed with a thud on her bottom, embarrassment heating her face.

She looked to her left, relieved to see the warriors were gathered in a circle around Brodee, not paying her any heed. She stood, shook out her gown, and then glanced to the right to search out Broch, but all she saw was an arrow coming directly at her. In the next breath, she was tackled to the ground from behind, but this time she ended up on her back with her husband on top of her.

Fear twisted his features for one moment before she felt his body tense and heard his teeth grind. "I told ye," he bit out, "to take a care."

This response was better, unless of course, he was only interested in how she made him look. She frowned and tried to concentrate on her plan. "And I told ye," she pushed at his chest to get him to move, "I have a horrid time making decisions, and presently, I need yer counsel."

He moved off her and brought her to her feet in one fluid motion, while also signaling for his men, who she previously had not seen up on a ledge to her right, to halt their practice.

"Is this life or death?" he growled.

"It could be," she replied, thinking he may well throttle her before this was over.

"What is it?" he demanded.

"I thought perhaps to wear my green gown tonight." She attempted to give him the most innocent look she could muster, but by the tic at his right eye, she knew he suspected she was trying to annoy him.

⁂

His sweet, complicated, plotting wife would be the death of him.

It had not taken long to realize what her strategy was in this game they were playing. She was attempting to get him to send her home. It was clever, and happened to be exactly what he wanted for her, but he wished it only temporarily, so she would be safe. But she seemed to want to return home in a plot to bend him to her will to live with her family or to allow her to aid him in seeking the person who pushed her off the cliff.

He would allow her several days to unfold her plan so she'd not suspect that he knew what she was doing, but he could not permit her to keep putting herself in danger. He hated having to be short with her, especially given the hurt he'd seen on her face earlier, but he had no choice.

He pointed a finger at her, to which she narrowed her eyes. "Dunnae," he said, making his tone purposely hard, "interrupt me again. In fact, dunnae do anything ye have even the slightest inkling may displease me."

"Or what?" she demanded, swatting his finger out of her face. He had to clench his teeth on a smile. His wee wife was a brave lass. Most men would not dare to stand up to him the way she did.

"Or," he said, bracing himself not to soften should she appear very wounded by his words, "I will take ye back to yer father's home, where ye will live out yer life without me."

"Dunnae make me too hopeful," she snapped. She swiveled on her heel and marched away.

He watched her flee, doubt battering him. Surely, she had not meant that. No, of course not. No woman would respond the way his wife just had after they had joined, nor would she wish to sever that connection for life. She was simply trying to get him to do as she desired.

He sighed. He could not even imagine what else she had concocted for the rest of the day, but he prayed it was nothing else that would put her in the path of danger. Anything would be better than that.

***

He'd been woefully wrong. Broch forced himself to remain seated at the dais in the great hall as his wife continued her plot to get him to send her home. It was the worst sort of torture he'd ever experienced to sit idly by and watch his wife flirt with other men—his men, men who should damn well know better than to talk so closely with his wife and look at her with such lust. He didn't know how much more he could take before he simply snapped and stormed into the crowd of Blackswell clansmen and women in the middle of the great hall, dancing and socializing.

He curled his hand around his goblet so tightly that he could feel the blood pulsing in his fingertips. Not once had he considered that her plot would involve making him jealous, and he was chagrined by how easily and powerfully his possessiveness had been stirred. He needed better control than this to make his wife believe he was delivering her to her home because she'd accomplished her goal.

A man Broch had not yet met, dark with a brooding look, approached his wife. She turned to him, and whatever he had said made her throw her head back and laugh in a hearty way that made Broch feel as if a fire had been lit inside him. He gritted his teeth as Brodee, whom Broch had confided in about the situation, leaned toward him. "If I were ye, I'd intercede now. Lasses seem to fall in love with Gavin Blackswell rather easily. Some of the men vow Esmerelda must have given Gavin a love potion."

"Ye're jesting, aye?" Broch asked, not looking at his brother because he didn't want to take his gaze off his wife.

"Nay," Brodee said. "His mother is the healer Esmerelda."

"I've nae met her." Broch clenched his jaw at the way Gavin Blackswell was staring lustfully at his wife. "It seems neither the healer nor her husband taught their son nae to covet what is another man's," Broch growled.

"Gavin's father is long dead," Brodee responded, then

leaned back and glanced to his right at their father. "Da, how did Esmerelda's husband die?" Broch looked at his father, waiting for him to answer.

Blackswell cleared his throat several times, then said, "He took ill and died before ever meeting his son. Verra sad really."

"Da gives Gavin too much leeway because of the loss of his father," Brodee said, scowling. "Gavin has bedded many a lass who belong to another man. If I had done such a thing, I'd be out of the clan."

Their father scowled. "Ye are the laird's son, first of all. Secondly, two people climb into a bed to sin. It is nae just Gavin's doing. When ye're older and have gained wisdom, ye'll see this."

"Far be it from me to tell ye how to rule," Brodee growled and shoved to his feet.

Broch stood, intending to tell his brother to stay and talk to their father, but when he looked to Brodee, he saw past him to the dance floor, where his wife danced entirely too close in Gavin Blackswell's arms. Heat flushed through his body, and his muscles tensed, as they often did before a battle. He ground his teeth as he strode from the dais without a word to his father or brother. It was time to end his wife's game.

Fifteen

Katreine saw Broch coming and she stumbled in the steps of the dance and careened into Gavin. He wrapped his arms about her waist to steady her, but he held her too tight and too long to simply ensure she was not going to fall. Before she could demand the man release her, Broch was there, glowering at her and Gavin.

"Unhand my wife." His thunderous tone made her flinch.

Gavin, to Katreine's dismay, pulled back his fist as if he was eager to fight Broch. The man was a fool. Actually, both men were fools. She'd not have danced with Gavin to stir Broch's jealousy if the man would just open up his eyes to the truth. She shoved away from Gavin, determined to take control of the situation. She wanted Broch to become angry and take her home, not kill this warrior.

"Thank ye for the dance," she told Gavin, then forced a smile. "But I'm tired now and wish to retire." It wasn't entirely a lie. She was tired and did wish to go to her bedchamber, but not to sleep. With the way things had been progressing with Broch, she wished to spend their time together giving him plenty of reasons to long for her return.

"I look forward to dancing with ye again, lass," Gavin said, then surprised her when he grasped her hand and started to draw it toward his lips. Broch's hand came to the man's wrist, and he turned it sharply. Gavin cried out, and before Katreine had time to even blink, Gavin was on his knees before her with his arm twisted up behind him.

Broch loomed over him, nostrils flaring and a vein throbbing at his neck. "Dunnae," he said very quietly, but the great hall was now silent so Katreine was certain everyone could hear anyway, "ever touch my wife again. This is a warning."

"And what will ye do if I dare it?" Gavin taunted, trying to twist back to look at Broch, but Broch jerked the man's arm higher behind him, and Gavin hissed in pain.

"Broch!" she cried out, dismayed her plan had led to this, but Broch did no more than spear a withering look at her before focusing on Gavin once more.

"I suggest," Broch growled, "that ye heed me so ye dunnae find out." With that, he released Gavin, grasped Katreine's arm—firmly but not so much so that it hurt her—and then with an arch of his eyebrows, he said, "I believe it's time for ye to go home."

"Now?" she gasped, her chest tightening and her breath accelerating.

He started striding toward the door, and she had no choice but to do so as well, lest she create a scene or stumble and fall. He paused as he passed Brodee, who stood talking to another warrior. "I need ye to accompany me to the Kinntochs'," Broch said to his brother. To her utter dismay, the two of them exchanged a knowing look as if they'd spoken of her. Broch was even now, on the verge of taking her away, choosing the Blackswells over her.

Her belly knotted, and she could not take a proper breath. This was the outcome she had desired, but she was hurt and shocked it had come so quickly. His feelings for her could not be very deep for him to be so easily driven to rid himself of her. And to add more hurt to the wound that was her aching heart, she had not imagined once that he would ask his brother to accompany him to return her home.

When the three of them proceeded out of the great hall door, Broch turned to her with his brother at his side. "Go gather whatever ye wish to take back home with ye. I'll send a servant to fetch it down while we—" he motioned between himself and his brother "—ready the horses."

The reality that she was leaving almost immediately began to sink in, and a sort of numbness began at her toes and spread rapidly to every part of her body. It was all she could do to nod, turn, and do as Broch had bade her. As she climbed the stairs, her mind raced through every moment since she'd met him, replaying each second from him rescuing her from Mungo, to their swim to the caves, to battling the wolves, to his Blackening and their wedding, to each and every smile, gentle touch, and rapturous joining. Had she been wrong about Broch? Did he not care for her the way she cared for him at all? If she looked back down the stairs now, and he was watching her, then he cared— and he was plotting something. If she glanced over her shoulder, and he was gone, then she'd made a fatal error in her plan for Broch because her plot had been dependent upon him feeling something special toward her.

She paused on the steps and stole a glance over her shoulder. Whatever thread of hope she had held on to snapped. He was gone. Tears welled in her eyes and her throat ached with the need to cry, but she rapidly blinked the tears away and swallowed repeatedly until she felt somewhat in control.

She trembled as she ascended the remaining steps. She

would not, under any circumstances, show the man he had hurt her. She would go home to her family and live just as she had originally planned. Except now, she knew without a doubt, that it could never be as she had thought. She had felt the possibility of love in her heart, and nothing would ever fill that void.

Four battle-ready warriors met Broch, Brodee, and Katreine at the drawbridge of her home. They were friendly and welcoming to Katreine, but they kept their eyes and swords pointed at Broch and Brodee. The Kinntoch warriors kept their weapons trained on them all the way to the great hall, where apparently the Kinntoch and his sons were gathered.

Katreine entered the room first, and as Broch followed with Brodee, he swept his gaze over Blackswell and Katreine's brothers, who were sitting at a table in front of the dais. Kinntoch and Donell were the first to rise. Donell slammed his wine goblet onto the table and swiped his palm across his mouth as Kinntoch said, "To what do we owe this visit?"

Before Broch could answer, Katreine swung around to face him, her head held high and her eyes twin pools of pain and swirling anger. "I'm being returned," she said, her voice low and her words halting. Broch had to clench his jaw on blurting the truth to Katreine. Seeing her hurt set an ache in him that was near unbearable.

"What say ye?" Kinntoch demanded.

Katreine faced her father, who was glaring at Broch, and she shrugged. "We could nae manage to live together peacefully, so now we will nae. May I return home?"

Broch fisted his hands to combat the pulsing need to

reach out to his wife and touch her, comfort her.

"Of course, Daughter," Kinntoch responded, but his gaze speared Broch. "Is this correct? Ye dunnae wish to have my daughter by yer side any longer?"

"That's correct," Broch managed, feeling gutted when Katreine's shoulders curled forward as if she were being battered by a storm.

"Father, I'd like to make my way to my chambers," Katreine asked.

"Aye, but one thing must be cleared first. Could there be a child?"

The very thought made Broch want to grin with happiness, but he ground his teeth together not to show the emotion.

"There could be," Katreine answered, not looking back at Broch. "And if there is, I'd like the child to live here with me."

"Nay," Broch responded. It was one thing to allow Katreine to think she'd won their battle for her own safety; it was quite another to allow her family to think, even for a breath, that they could keep his heir.

She swung toward Broch once more, looking now like a glorious, enraged angel. "So ye dunnae want me, but ye think to take my bairn from me?" Before he could answer her question about a child that may not even exist yet, she yanked out her dagger and pointed it at him. "Ye will nae part me from my bairn ever! I'll see ye, or anyone who dares to try, dead." With that, she stormed past him and out of the great hall, slamming the door behind her.

Broch grinned with pride, noted Kinntoch and Katreine's brothers all giving him odd looks, and then he said, "My wife is a bold lass! She dunnae have fear, Kinntoch." He laughed when the man gaped at him. "I'm thankful for the excellent woman ye raised," he added.

Brodee leaned over to him. "I think we should mayhap explain."

"Aye," Donell and Kinntoch replied as one.

"Before we kill ye," Donell added.

Broch took a deep breath and began to tell them the long tale of all that had transpired—and of his plan.

For the first few days after leaving Katreine in the safety of her home, Broch divided his time between training his men and questioning as many Blackswells as he could. He had to discover who had pushed Katreine off the cliff and murdered Arabel and Lenora. He did so with Brodee's help, but to both of their frustrations, they did not uncover any new evidence.

Broch's desire to go collect his wife was already making him testy, and it showed in his training. He was short with his men, and when his father brought Gavin to Broch's group and informed Broch that he'd promoted Gavin to be one of Broch's personal guards, his irritation ratcheted up to near boiling.

His jealousy over Gavin touching his wife had resulted in Broch foolishly taking Katreine home earlier than he'd planned. He had intended to travel back with her to Thioram the day after the incident and had hoped to share a tender joining to ease the hurt she'd undoubtedly feel when he left her. And now that the man was before him, looking arrogant, Broch wanted to decimate him on the training field. The logical side of his mind knew that it was his own damn fault he'd allowed his possessiveness to make him act in haste, but he wanted to blame someone for the separation from Katreine he was being forced to endure. And at the moment, since he was no closer to finding the murderer among them, Gavin seemed the perfect person to lay the fault at his feet.

Yet, as he summoned the warrior into the training ring, he recalled what Katreine had said when they'd first met: all Blackswells were dishonorable, despicable men. If he unleashed his anger at himself and his circumstances upon Gavin, he would be proving his wife correct, when he was in the mess because he'd set out to prove her wrong about his family.

With a sigh, he motioned Gavin closer, vowing to teach, not torture. "Show me what ye can do," he said, and before he could step back to raise his sword, the man launched an attack. Gavin thrust his sword toward Broch's stomach, which Broch barely avoided by jumping backward.

"This is training, ye daft fool!" Brodee yelled at Gavin.

Broch shook his head at his brother for silence, even as he parried Gavin's blows, first on the left and then the right. The man had skill and a lot of anger, which all seemed to be directed at Broch, likely for the humiliation he'd endured at Broch's hands. For that, Broch would give Gavin this one opportunity to try to best him.

"Ye wish me to restrain myself with ye?" Gavin snarled at Broch, catching him across the arm with his blade, which cut easily into his skin.

Broch gritted his teeth and shook his head. "Give me all ye have, and I'll show ye why it's nae enough."

That seemed to further enrage Gavin. He turned nearly purple in the face and swung his sword toward Broch's neck. Broch ducked, came up, and caught Gavin on the leg, but drew his sword back before it could do real damage.

Gavin let out a guttural sound. "I'm nae afraid of ye, Blackswell's eldest son," he boomed. "I'll send ye back to yer maker, aye."

"My lord," several of Broch's men called out, their worry at Gavin's threat apparent. Even Brodee stepped toward Gavin.

Broch shouted, "Hold," at his brother, who stilled, appearing pained at following the command.

"I'm nae quite ready to meet my maker," Broch responded to Gavin, dodging another jab of the man's sword. But this time, he swiveled back into it and knocked Gavin's weapon with such force that it went flying out of the man's hands and landed at Brodee's feet.

Brodee promptly kneeled, picked it up, and stepped toward Gavin, who now stood still with his palms up in the sign of surrender. Brodee pointed the sword at Gavin's chest. "I should gut ye for threatening my brother."

Broch yanked Brodee back and gave him a nod of thanks before addressing Gavin. "I ken ye're vexed with me for the incident in the great hall the other night. I'll nae apologize, as ye likely want. Ye touched my wife. Dunnae do so again."

The man glared at him, a vein pulsing near his right eye. "Ye think she's too good for me to dance with because I'm nae one of the laird's sons?" Gavin snapped.

It was easy for Broch to spot a man who felt he had something to prove, who felt he was somehow lesser, because Broch had been such a man. A shaft of pity stabbed him, but that did not mean he was about to excuse Gavin for openly trying to woo Katreine.

"I think my wife is too good for me," Broch countered, "so aye, I believe she is too good for ye, as well. But since luck let *me* wed her, she is mine to keep and protect. I dunnae share what is mine. *Ever.* And if ye kinnae accept that, then we will have a true quarrel."

"As ye wish," the man snarled before turning on his heel and striding away.

Brodee came to stand by Broch. "That's a man with something to prove."

"Aye," Broch acknowledged, thinking of his own past. "It's being raised fatherless, I think. I'll keep my eye on him."

"As will I, Brother," Brodee promised as the supper bell rang. Brodee slung his arm over Broch's shoulder. "Shall we sup?"

Broch nodded, and they made their way into the great hall. As they entered, Broch noted a willowy woman with long black hair sitting at the dais, speaking to their father. She was seated at Broch's place. "Who is that?" Broch asked.

"'Tis the healer, Esmerelda. Gavin's mother. She birthed us."

"Aye," Broch replied. "I ken. The bard told me. She's verra beautiful."

"At one time I thought perhaps Da might take up with her, but though he speaks with her often, he is distant with her."

Broch watched his father, who appeared almost uncomfortable as he spoke to the healer. "Did ye ever ask him about it?"

"Oh, aye," Brodee replied. "He said not in this life or the next could any woman replace our mother."

The two men stood there for a moment, grinning at each other, and for the first time in his life, Broch felt at home. It would be perfect when Katreine was by his side once more. Thinking of her made him ponder what his father had said. "I can understand that," Broch said. "I kinnae imagine ever taking another wife if Katreine died."

"Already?" Brodee teased.

"Aye, Brother. Already," Broch replied, not minding speaking of this to his brother. He was, after all, the elder brother giving advice to the younger one. "One day ye will meet a lass and ye will ken what I am saying. When she is the right lass, ye will ken it. And when that space inside ye reserved for the special woman has been filled, there is simply nae filling it with another."

Brodee and Broch started toward the dais, and as they did, the healer scampered away without a backward glance. "Is she always so friendly?" Broch asked sarcastically.

"Aye," Brodee said with a chuckle. "She's an odd one."

They both greeted their father, and once they were settled, they turned to him and asked for stories of their mother almost in unison. All three of them burst out laughing, and they sat there for a great long time, listening to Blackswell tell them of their mother's love of riding and swimming, and all things her father and mother had not thought fit for a lass, which was why she had run away. Broch drank liberally of his wine—and Brodee's when Brodee said he was not thirsty—though the spirits were a bit sour for Broch's taste. He had not been able to sleep since he'd left Katreine at her father's home, and tonight, he simply wanted to sink into oblivion and start fresh tomorrow.

By the time dinner was over, his head and mouth felt as if they were filled with sheep's wool, and he was seeing double of his brother and father, who finally seemed to be communicating. "I'm to bed," he said, pushing up from the bench, but when he did, the room swayed before him. He tilted to the right, grabbed at the table to steady himself, and accidentally knocked Brodee's wine goblet off the table. Red immediately stained Brodee's plaid.

"I'm sorry, Brother," Broch said, intending to say more, but something was pounding inside his head as if trying to escape it by cracking it in two. And a sharp pain came at his side, then in his stomach. "I think I'm dying," he moaned, his brother and father swimming in and out of his vision.

As if from a long tunnel, he heard Brodee say, "God's teeth! He's been poisoned. Touch the wine to yer tongue, Father. 'Tis Widow's Malice!"

"Poisoned," Broch mumbled. "Aye." He swayed again but knew instinctually he was going to fall into the pit of fire that had consumed his body. "Tell Katreine I loved her," he managed to say before he crashed backward into darkness.

Sixteen

"Katreine!" Cadyn called as he pounded at her bedchamber door. "Ye're wanted in the great hall."

"Leave me be!" She pulled her blanket more securely over her head. It had been four days since Broch had left her here, but it felt like a lifetime. She missed him terribly, and she feared she'd made a grave mistake. Why had she embarked on such a ludicrous plan? She could have eventually shown him the truth of his family while there.

"Katreine," Cadyn said as the door to her bedchamber squeaked open.

She sat up in the bed and glared at her brother. "Go away, Cadyn," she said, though she knew her kindhearted brother only meant well.

He'd tried several times over the last few days to speak with her and reassure her that Broch would return. Even Donell had been restrained around her, not talking ill of Broch and going so far as to say he considered her husband a MacLeod at heart. She had no idea what had prompted Donell to make such a statement, especially given how he'd acted toward Broch during the Blackening ceremony. Or maybe it was because of the Blackening ceremony and the honor and strength Broch had shown that Donell had realized Broch was a good man.

Her bed dipped as Cadyn sat beside her, a grave look

upon his face. "Ye must dress now. Father says ye're to come to the great hall immediately. Brodee Blackswell is here to see ye."

Katreine frowned. "Brodee? But nae Broch?"

Cadyn carefully avoided her gaze, which alerted her immediately that something was afoot. God's teeth. Had Broch sent his brother to say he did nae ever wish to see her again? "Is he here on Broch's behalf?"

"In a sense."

"Oh God!" she wailed. "I'm such a fool. I—"

"Katreine, Broch was poisoned," Cadyn interrupted.

"What?" Her mind reeled at the news, and when her brother nodded, she trembled with horrible fear. "He's nae—" She swallowed. "I mean to ask, is he—

"He's alive, Sister," Cadyn said gently.

Such relief filled her that tears welled in her eyes and spilled down her cheeks. Normally, she would never show such weakness to her brothers or father, but presently, she simply did not care. Then another thought hit that had her reaching for the dagger that was sheathed at Cadyn's hip.

He stayed her movements with his hand upon her wrist. "What are ye doing?" he demanded.

"I'm going to kill Brodee," she replied, rage now boiling in her as she tried to jerk away from her brother's hold, but his grip became unrelenting.

"Brodee did nae poison Broch. He has been working with yer husband to discover who murdered Lenora and Brodee's leman and who pushed ye off the cliff at Hightower."

She startled. "How did ye ken I was pushed?"

"When Broch brought ye home and ye marched upstairs in a huff, he told us about ye being pushed off the cliff, and then Brodee told us of seeing Lenora the day she died, what they spoke of, and how he had left her vexed."

She frowned. "And ye simply believed him?"

"Nay," her brother said, giving her a stern look. "But he did nae have anything to gain by being dishonest, and more importantly, Broch believes him, and I trust in yer husband."

"I do, too," she said hotly, but then she froze. God's bones, none of her actions had shown her trust or her belief in Broch. She had shown him the opposite. She scrambled off the bed. "I have to go to him."

"Aye, ye do. Brodee says Broch was verra sick last night and would have died if nae for the healer Esmerelda, who created a cure for the poison he'd been given."

She tugged on her slippers, then stood and looked at her brother. "Does everyone else believe Brodee's innocence?"

"Aye, especially because when they left ye here, Broch told us he was doing so to keep ye safe, and that he and Brodee planned to question all Blackswells again. Upon coming here this morning, Brodee even offered to return the half of Derthshire his family received for yer marriage to Broch, if we will help them find the real murderer."

"Our families are at peace?" she asked, stupefied but thankful.

"Aye. Finally, after so long hating each other." He met her gaze. "Are ye prepared to forgive, Sister?"

She nodded and then headed out the door to see Brodee. She was prepared to forgive and to aid her husband, whether he wished it or not, in discovering who poisoned him. He was not the only one determined to protect. She wanted to protect him, too. She wanted his love, and to give him hers.

She made her way to the great hall, her face heating as she saw Brodee. She had been so awful to him. "I'm sorry," she said simply, walking toward him as she nodded to her father and brothers.

Brodee shoved back a lock of his hair and smiled, which looked truly genuine as it lit his blue eyes. "As am I," he said. "If I'd been truthful from the start, and we had nae coveted the land all those years—"

"Bygones," she inserted, looking to her father and Donell, who nodded their agreement. "How is Broch?" Her chest tightened just asking the question. Heavens, he could have died!

"Recovering and grouchy. He dunnae ken I'm here to fetch ye."

"Oh." She bit her lip in consternation. "Mayhap he will nae be happy that ye have come for me."

Brodee grinned mischievously. "He will nae, to be certain, but I believe ye will help him heal more quickly."

"Me? I'm nae a healer."

"I ken, but the last thing he said before he passed out last night was, 'Tell Katreine I loved her.'" A cry of relief broke from her lips, at which Brodee smiled. "I thought this would please ye." He looked at her knowingly. "I believe if he hears the same from ye, he may heal more quickly."

She gave her brother and her father a stern look. "All is forgiven, aye?"

"Aye," they both agreed.

Her father cleared his throat and said, "We will leave half of Derthshire with the Blackswells so both clans may prosper."

"Thank ye, Father!" she said, feeling a peace she had not felt in years. "Come." She grasped Brodee's arm. "My husband needs me at our home."

It was an all-day journey, but when she entered their bedchamber late that night, Broch was snoring soundly. Even in sleep, her husband looked every inch the indomitable warrior. His thick arms rested on his hips, and he gripped his sword in one hand and a dagger in the other. He wore only his braies, but he had two more daggers sheathed and in ready reach. She leaned down, wanting very badly to touch him, to run her hands over the solid length of his long Viking legs, and over the corded muscle of his chest, but she did not want to wake him. He was a legend, but then so was Achilles. Even men who seemed indestructible could be felled, and her husband almost had been—by poison.

Tears welled in her eyes, and she blinked, causing some drops to land on Broch's face. Instantly, his eyelids flew open. He looked baffled for a moment, and then his eyes narrowed dangerously. "What are ye doing here?" he growled.

She pried his fingers from his sword, arching her eyebrows at him when he would not relent. Finally, with a grunt, he released his weapons to her but indicated that she should lay them on the bed, which she did on his right side so she could lie beside him on his left. She rolled onto her side and reached an arm over his chest to hold him while she settled her cheek against his shoulder. She slid her hand to his heart, grateful for the strong beat beneath her fingertips. She glanced up at him and was not surprised to find his keen gaze watching her.

"I'm here," she said, "because I love ye, just as I ken ye love me, and," she rushed on when he looked as though he was about to protest, "ye need me to protect ye, just as I need ye to protect me. And the best way for us to do that is together."

He opened and closed his mouth several times before

he said, "Either ye are a fool for disobeying me or ye are unaccountably reckless." She knew by the tenderness in his eyes and the love shining there that she would win this particular battle to stay by her husband's side. She pushed herself up toward his face and brushed her lips to his warm ones. "I'm a fool—*for ye*," she murmured.

"'Tis good." He slanted his mouth over hers, only breaking the kiss to say, "Because I'm a fool for ye, as well." He held her face in his hands. "I love ye, lass. I think I fell the day I met ye."

Her heart squeezed at his words. "I love ye, too, and I am certain I fell the day I met ye." He kissed her forehead, her nose, her cheeks, and then her mouth. His hands started to pull up her skirts, but she leaned back. "Ye are recovering from being poisoned," she said sternly.

"Aye." A glint came to his eyes. "But there is nae any better medicine than yer touch."

"In that case," she said wickedly, coming to her knees and drawing her simple gown over her head, "love me."

"Always," he replied, sitting up and sliding his hands under her loose léine to cup her breasts.

Her heart sang with delight as he began to work his magic upon her body, teasing her nipples until they ached with the flicks and circles of his tongue. And then he took the hard buds in his mouth and suckled with long pulls that made her temporarily lose coherent thought. Soon, her body was on fire with need for her husband, and she thought to make their joining quick, since he'd been ill, but he clearly had a different plan.

He undressed them both slowly, his gaze worshiping her even as his hands and mouth did. He trailed kisses between the valley of her breasts, over her quivering belly, and between her thighs, which he gently parted. He ignited her need to her very core with lavish slides of his tongue to her most intimate parts, making her scream and rake at his back. And when he began to make her frenzied, as he had before with his wicked mouth, she tugged his head up. "'Tis my turn."

His eyebrows shot up with his surprise. "Do ye mean—"

"Aye, Husband," she purred, enjoying his look of astonishment, followed swiftly by eager anticipation. She felt suddenly powerful. "Lie on yer back."

"I'm yers to command, Wife," he responded in a lazy, seductive voice.

And in this moment, he was, because he allowed it, because he trusted her. Nothing could have made her feel stronger or more loved than that. She first took the length of him in her hands, touching him hesitantly, but by his eager grunts, she began to discover what he liked. When she felt more confidant, she took him in her mouth. His body tensed, and then his hands fisted in her hair as he let out a guttural moan, emboldening her to show him the same attention he'd shown her earlier. Soon, her warrior husband was like clay in her hands, and excitement raced through her as she brought him to the same heights to which he had taken her.

When she was finished, she lay back, assuming he'd be sated and fulfilled, but he hovered over her, brought his hands under her buttocks, and slid into her. He filled her completely and perfectly, and together they began to move in a rhythm only the two of them would ever share. Soon, her heart pounded, her breath came in gasps, and she cried out, clenching his torso between her thighs. But Broch was not one to give mercy. He slowed his strokes, making her growl at him, and then increased them once more, until her body, tight as a coil, sprang and gave way to the warmth of bliss only he could bring her.

Afterward, she lay with her cheek resting on his chest, and her leg over his. "Who do ye think poisoned ye?" she asked in the darkness of their chamber.

"I dunnae ken, but tomorrow, I intend to seek out the bard once again and see if he recalls any stories of old that might shed light on the ongoing problems. Do ye wish to accompany me?"

She grinned up at him. "I wish to thank Esmerelda. Yer brother told me how she made a cure for ye."

"Aye, 'tis what he told me, as well. I've nae had a chance to thank her. I'll likely be gone most of the morning. I'd like ye nae to walk the grounds, if ye will be so kind as to oblige."

She loved him so much for asking and not demanding. "I will stay in the castle. I vow it."

Seventeen

"Ye're grinning like a fool," Brodee said to Broch as they rode through the woods.

The bard's cottage appeared up ahead, and Broch brought his horse to a stop and looked over at his brother, who had insisted on going with Broch to ensure he was fit for the journey. He grinned as he thought of his joining with Katreine that morning. Oh, he definitely had the strength to ride his horse.

"It's certain. Marriage has made ye a clot-heid," Brodee teased with a roll of his eyes.

"Aye, it has," Broch agreed happily. "I'm a clot-heid for my wife. And ye're jealous."

There was a time, not long ago, Broch would not have said such a thing to Brodee, but things were well between them, and Brodee had told Broch on the journey today that he had spoken to their father as they had both watched over Broch in the night. Their father had asked for forgiveness for the distance he'd put between them and for being so critical of Brodee, and had begged for them to start over. Broch could not have been more pleased. Everything he'd wanted was in the palms of his hands. That familiar sense of wariness that something would be snatched from him overcame him, as did the urge to see the bard immediately and discover if he had any valuable information.

"Come," Broch said, setting his horse to a trot and not waiting for Brodee to respond. Broch did not lessen his pace until he was almost at the bard's door. He dismounted quickly and knocked, hearing Brodee approach behind him. As Brodee came to stand beside him, Alban opened the door.

His silver eyebrows raised over wise eyes creased with many lines. "What brings the two of ye to me this day?" His voice crackled like a dying fire.

"We are hoping ye might recall some stories from the time we were born," Broch said, motioning between himself and Brodee.

"I dunnae think I ken any that ye would nae already have heard from Blackswell, but I'll tell ye what I can recall." Alban gestured them inside.

They entered the small, one-room cottage, and Alban indicated two chairs. "Take a seat," he said, then hobbled to the hearth and slowly lowered himself to the ledge, his joints cracking as he sat. Inhaling deeply, the old man placed his hands, the skin looking almost paper-thin, upon his knees. "What do ye seek to ken, so I may understand the best stories to recall?"

Brodee and Broch exchanged a quick look, and then, as if by a silent agreement, Broch spoke. "We seek to find the person responsible for murdering Arabel and Lenora."

Brodee quickly reminded the bard who the two women were, and then Broch continued. "And more recently, my wife, Katreine, was pushed from the ledge where her sister died. Katreine lived, but we think the same person who pushed her likely murdered the two women."

Alban scratched at his beard for a long moment, then looked between the two brothers. "I'm an old man now, aye, but let me see…" The man looked as if he were gazing through a window to the past. "There was once a powerful laird known throughout the land for his prowess."

Brodee chuckled. "That would be our father in his youth," to which Alban glared at him.

"Dunnae interrupt," the bard instructed in firm tone.

Brodee quickly nodded.

"The laird had many lovers," Alban went on, "until one particular woman, a healer with hair the cover of a black night, bewitched him."

Broch frowned. He only knew one healer—Esmerelda. But surely, the bard was not referring to her. "What was this leman's name?" he asked.

Alban scowled at him. "Do the two of ye wish to hear my story or nae?"

"Aye," the brothers both answered.

And then Broch said, "But—"

"Esmerelda," Alban snapped.

Broch glanced to Brodee, who looked as shocked as Broch felt. Esmerelda had been their father's leman. Of course, their father had told Broch that he and their mother had argued because Blackswell had refused to send his leman away, but Broch had assumed he eventually had.

"As I was saying, the healer mesmerized the laird. Some said she was *ban-druidh*." Alban cackled at that. "She is nae a witch," he assured them both. "Just a woman who kenned well how to pleasure a man. But there is pleasure of the body and then joy of the heart." He touched a finger to his chest. "The great laird went to a summer tourney and met a lass with lavender eyes, who brought him first joy to his heart and later, after they wed, pleasure to his body. He was enraptured, and all was perfect in the land. But all kinnae stay perfect. 'Tis nae nature's way. Nature gives and takes away."

Broch tensed, reminded of his fear that something he'd always wanted and only recently found was going to be taken from him.

"The laird brought his new wife back to Hightower, but when he did, he discovered his leman carried his child, forcing him to tell his wife about Esmerelda."

Broch's gut tightened, and a suspicion rose in him.

"It put distance between the laird and his wife," the bard said, "because she was naturally jealous, even though the laird did nae ever touch Esmerelda again in lust. Esmerelda was furious to be spurned by Blackswell, but she had confidence that once their bairn was born, Blackswell would return to her bed."

Broch's fingers curled around the hilt of his sheathed dagger as his heart began to pound.

"Then Blackswell's new bride's belly began to swell with his heirs—the two of ye—even as Esmerelda's belly swelled."

Broch shifted, thinking suddenly how Esmerelda had been near the dais the night he was poisoned and thinking of Gavin's hatred of him. The strong desire to go to Katreine filled him, but he had to hear the rest of the story to be certain his suspicion was true.

"When Esmerelda's wee lass was born, she was nae living."

Broch sucked in a sharp breath.

"Esmerelda was crazed and plotted to get the laird back. She blamed her bairn's death and losing Blackswell on yer mother. Yer mother, in turn, demanded he send Esmerelda away, but I think his guilt and pride would nae allow him to do so. So it was on the day ye two were born that yer father and mother were nae speaking."

The bard sat back as if he were done, and Brodee and

Broch spoke in unison again. "That's it?"

"Well, much of the rest of what I could tell ye I've gotten in bits and pieces from Esmerelda's sister Nesa and the clanswomen who heard whisperings. I did nae see or hear it myself, so I dunnae like to repeat it."

"Tell us," Broch urged, the feeling that something bad was about to happen increasing.

Alban looked as if he would argue, but after a moment, he nodded. "Esmerelda's sister shared with me that Esmerelda demanded Nesa lie for her."

"What lie did Esmerelda want Nesa to tell?" Brodee prodded, his hands in fists upon his knees.

"According to Nesa, on the day yer mother gave birth to ye, Esmerelda had Nesa tell yer mother that Blackswell was still bedding Esmerelda."

"Father thinks Nesa told Mother to be hateful to Esmerelda. I believe he thinks Esmerelda had nothing to do with it," Broch said.

"We can solve this by asking Nesa herself, but I dunnae ken her," Brodee said. "Where does she now live Alban?"

"She died," the bard said. "'Twas a stomach ailment that took her suddenly, the day after ye were born."

A black certainty gripped Broch's heart, and when he looked to Brodee, whose lips were pressed in a thin line, he knew they were both thinking the same thing: Esmerelda had poisoned her sister and likely had poisoned him, too.

"There is nae much left to this story," Alban said. "Blackswell's wife fled him the day after she gave birth to two braw sons. She took the oldest with her." Alban looked to Broch. "And the youngest by a breath," Alban said, glancing to Brodee, "she left in Nesa's care, but when Nesa died, Esmerelda thought to make ye almost as her own bairn, I think. 'Tis only my conjecture. But Blackswell was grieved and guilty over what he had done to cause his wife to leave and take his eldest heir. He took the bairn he had left and kept him close, even as he kept Esmerelda at a distance."

"And what whisperings did ye hear of what Esmerelda did next?" Broch demanded, his blood roaring in his ears. He would have every detail when he confronted the woman.

"She wed another, but the womenfolk talked of how she hated him. I think perhaps he was cruel, and she bemoaned the lot fate had given her. She thought she should have been the laird's wife, and him keeping her here kept that hope alive. 'Tis all I ken. The two of ye must go away now. I'm old and tired."

Broch stood, very eager to return to the castle. All he could think of was that Katreine had intended to go see Esmerelda. God's teeth, he prayed Katreine was unharmed.

When the door closed behind Broch and Brodee, Broch turned to his brother. "Do ye think—"

"That Esmerelda is the murderer?" Brodee finished. "Aye."

"We have to ride hard and fast," Broch said, mounting his horse. "Katreine intended to visit the healer. If anything happens..." Broch could not finish the sentence. He could not even think of losing her. She was his home, his family.

※

Katreine knocked on the healing room door, which had taken her several attempts to find. The healing room was technically part of the castle, but it was set apart from the main keep, joined to it by a bridge to which the stairs had been difficult to locate. She waited a minute, and when no one answered, she pushed open the door and stuck her head in the room, deciding she would remain until the healer returned. One of the kitchen girls had told Katreine that Esmerelda had been headed toward her healing room the last she'd seen her, which had been moments before Katreine had asked where she could find it. Something or someone must have detained the woman.

She glanced around the sunlit room, drawn to the shelves packed with herbs, spices, and bowls, and she began to sift through them, sniffing and peering. The healing arts appealed to her greatly. Perhaps she could persuade the healer to teach her. Incense floated into the air in a white, spiral trail, and when she leaned close to smell it, she bumped a table. A box fell off the table, and its contents spilled onto the floor.

She glanced at the door behind her, embarrassed, and kneeled down to gather the fallen objects before Esmerelda returned. After she had everything back in the heavy, bejeweled box, she went to pick it up, but a stone sliced her finger open, making her almost drop it again. She grabbed it before it fell and started to turn it right side up, but when her thumb pressed against the bottom of the box, a small compartment popped open and a ring fell out. It hit her shoe, and she bent down to get it.

She froze. Sheer black fright blew through her like a storm as she pinched her sister's long-lost emerald ring between her thumb and forefinger. Her heart pounded a deafening beat as she stood and brought the ring close to her face to look at it. She would have known this ring anywhere. It was a large emerald set on an unusual gold-twined band.

Her mind began to race, filled with thoughts and questions. Why did the healer have it? Had Esmerelda found it, or had she killed Lenora? And why? Why would she kill Lenora? Why would—

"Gavin, no!" came a woman's voice from behind her.

Katreine whirled toward the voice, but all she saw was the hilt of a dagger coming toward her. The hit sent her reeling backward and snuffed out all the light.

Broch strode toward the stairs that led to Esmerelda's room with Brodee and their father close behind. They'd encountered him moments before when they'd entered the keep, and as they made their way to the stairwell, Brodee had told Blackswell all they had learned from Alban. Broch did not bother to knock at Esmerelda's door. He turned the handle, intent on barging in, but found it locked. He knocked, and when no answer came, he stepped back and kicked the door inward. It flew open with a bang on the inner wall to reveal Esmerelda lying on the ground, unmoving.

"God's teeth!" Broch thundered, stunned.

He, Brodee, and Blackswell crouched as one and rolled Esmerelda from her side to her back. Blood streaked her forehead, and Broch could see she had been hit. He looked around for something to press to the cut and stilled. A ring glittered near the woman's head. He picked it up, a memory stirring, and held it out to Brodee. "Is this—"

"Aye," Brodee interrupted. "'Tis Lenora's ring."

"God's bones," Blackswell muttered. "What the devil is happening?"

"I dunnae ken, but I'm going to find out," Broch ground out, worry for Katreine gnawing at him. He'd come straight here, so maybe, *maybe* she'd not come to see Esmerelda. Maybe she was in their bedchamber. "Wake up," he said, shaking the healer.

After several attempts, Blackswell said, "Let me try." Broch moved to let Blackswell crouch before the healer.

"Esmerelda, 'tis me, Blackswell. Open yer eyes, please." After a long pause, the woman slowly opened her eyes, looking confused at first, and then when her gaze focused on Blackswell, she gasped and tried to scramble backward. He gripped her wrist and held her still. "What have ye done, woman?" She pressed her lips into a thin line, and Blackswell gripped her by the shoulders, his face twisting with anger. "Tell me what ye have done, or so help me—"

"Ye'll what?" she rasped. "Force me to wed the captain of yer guard again? Who will beat me until I submit my body, which I was saving for ye!"

Broch flinched at that revelation, as did Blackswell, whose lips parted in shock. "I did nae ken," Blackswell said. "I only thought to give ye a good life."

"Ye were my life!" she cried. "Ye took yerself away from me and replaced me with that *woman!*" Her accusing gaze swerved to Broch and Brodee. "My bairn died because of her!"

"Nay, Esmerelda," Blackswell said, sagging.

"Aye!" she insisted. "But then I had another—Gavin. I wanted him to be yers so badly. I wanted to be yers. That *ban-druidh* was gone—"

"By yer doing!" Brodee thundered.

"Aye," Esmerelda agreed, her lips turning up. "By my doing!"

Blackswell swore.

"Still, ye would nae come to me," Esmerelda continued. "Nae touch me. Ye mourned for her, while all I wanted was to give ye Gavin to raise as yer own! Oh, but nae until I made ye hate her son so ye would replace Gavin with him. I whispered in yer ear how he was to blame, and ye grew distant but nae enough. I had Gavin kill to make Brodee appear a murderer, and still ye clung to yer love for him!"

"By God, Esmerelda, I'll kill ye!" Blackswell roared.

"Nay!" Broch shouted. "Katreine," he reminded his father. "Have ye seen her? Esmerelda? Has my wife been here?"

"Here and gone," she said, waving her hand. "Gavin, the fool, took her to kill her. I tried to warn him that it was too soon, that we'd be discovered, but he wants his father's love so badly," she crowed, sounding demented. Her gaze bore into Blackswell's. "He is yers," she announced.

"We did nae ever lay together again, woman!" Blackswell thundered.

She shrugged. "It dunnae matter. In my mind and heart, he is yers, and he thinks he is yers. He would have gotten Derthshire for ye with more time to continue the raids. He killed for ye, Blackswell!"

Broch crouched low and pressed his face near Esmerelda's. "Where the devil did yer spawn take my wife?"

"To the caves on her land. He'll slit her throat," she said in a pleasant tone as if discussing the weather. "And the Kinntochs will think ye did it." She stared at Broch. "They will rise against us, and then Blackswell will have his land."

"Ye are mad!" Broch said, rising as a tremor went through his body. "I have to—"

"It will be too late!" she crowed. "Ye will be too late to save her! In the end, we all suffer for yer fickle heart, Blackswell."

Blackswell's hands were fisted at his side, his expression enraged. "My heart belonged to my wife from the moment I laid eyes upon her, and it always will."

Broch made for the door, footfalls at his heels. He

turned to find Brodee behind him, and Blackswell dragging Esmerelda to her feet. "Go," Blackswell said. "I will see to Esmerelda, as I should have done years ago."

Broch nodded and strode out the door. Brodee sped up to walk beside him. "Katreine is nae called the Hellion of the Highlands for naught, Broch. If anyone can survive this, 'tis yer wife."

Broch could do no more than nod.

Eighteen

Katreine awoke to darkness. The salty smell of the sea mingled with the smoky smell of a fire, and the crashing of the water upon the rocks intertwined with the crackling and popping of burning wood. Slowly, she opened her eyes to find Gavin crouched on the other side of a fire, staring at her.

She sat up, glancing around, and realized he had brought her to the caves she knew well. He held a dagger in his hand, and suddenly, he smiled. "I'm to kill ye," he said in a voice so devoid of emotion that she shivered.

The urge to run nearly overwhelmed her, but she felt certain there would only be one chance to escape and she needed to take a care. "Why?" she asked, striving to keep her own tone as devoid of emotion as his had been.

"'Tis simple, really. If we eliminate everyone who stands in our way, Da will love me and Mother."

"Da?" Katreine asked, eyeing the dagger sheathed at his hip. Could she grasp that dagger and plunge it into his black heart?

"Blackswell," Gavin answered, shocking her. "Blackswell is my father. I'll be the heir when yer husband and Brodee are gone."

Her mind was reeling with what he was saying. She had no notion if any of it was true. It didn't matter. All that mattered was surviving to return to Broch. "Did ye kill my sister?" Katreine asked, her heart squeezing with memories and a fresh sense of loss.

"Aye," he said. "'Twas necessary so that Blackswell would turn from Brodee, but he didn't." The man's face clouded over, and Katreine had an idea.

"I can help ye. Killing me will only make Broch and Blackswell think Brodee is a murderer, but ye will still have to contend with Broch."

"I plan to," Gavin said. "I poisoned him once, but my mother gave in to Blackswell's pleas of her aid to make a cure. I'll ensure she dunnae do that again. I dunnae need yer aid."

Her breath seemed to have solidified in her throat. She swallowed and then forced out her words. "My family will declare war upon Blackswell if I am killed, and mayhap kill him and ye. If ye let me live, we could wed after ye kill Broch and be family. All of us." Her words made her feel ill.

"Ye would wed me?" he asked, intrigue underlying the question.

Sweat trickled down her back as her head pounded. "Aye. To live I would do anything."

He chuckled at that. "Ye really are a hellion!" he said. "I like that. Ye say ye will do anything to live?"

Dread filled her gut. "Aye," she croaked.

"Lay with me." His gaze raked over her from head to foot so that her stomach knotted with disgust. "Willingly," he added. "I want ye willing and showing me just how much better I am than yer husband, *the eldest son*," he snarled.

Rage filled her. Oh, she was going to show him something, to be certain. "All right," she said, rising to stand, so he did as well. Without a word, she undid her laces and tugged off her gown as her heart beat so hard it hurt her chest.

"'Tis yer turn." She pointed at his plaid.

He grinned, grasped his plaid, and raised his hands to pull it over his broad shoulders. The moment his vison was obscured by the plaid, she dived toward him, grabbed the dagger sheathed at his hip, and drove it forward, intent on piercing his heart. But he smacked her hand, and the dagger struck his arm, lodging there instead.

He bellowed with rage, and she bolted past him toward the cave opening. She stumbled out of the cave, panic making her slower than she had intended. His footsteps thudded behind her as she ran toward the rocks and the water. He'd outrun her in the woods. The water was her only hope. She just prayed she was not towed under by the pull of the waves.

"Katreine!" Gavin roared, and she dove into the water.

―❦―

Broch spotted Gavin running in the moonlight from the cave, just as the man roared Katreine's name. Broch frantically searched the moonlit night for Katreine, and then he saw her, diving into the very waters she had once warned him were dangerous.

"Go to her!" Brodee shouted. "I'll see to Gavin!"

Broch did not even answer. No breath could be wasted. Every one was for his wife. Brodee ran past him and barreled into Gavin as Broch made for the rock ledge and dove into the water after Katreine. Cold stole his breath and blackness stole his sight, but it didn't matter. Nothing mattered but finding her.

He moved his arms wildly in front of him, praying for a

touch of her body, but there was nothing but endless, unforgiving ocean. He was tossed up to the surface only to be dragged back under. Water filled his nose, his mouth; his lungs burned. His mind felt as if it was going to explode, and the hunger for air clawed at him as it must be clawing at Katreine.

He swam forward, instead of up. She was his life. She made his family complete. He had to save her. A wave grabbed him once more and threw him into a rock. Sharp edges cut down his back as he was yanked below again, but then something grazed his foot and clasped his ankle.

Katreine!

Even as he bent for her, she reached for him, and they came body to body, pressed together as one, being tumbled in the ocean. As he gripped her, hope and fear battered him. They had to make the surface, but how? She clamped a hand on his arm and seemed to tug him, so he followed, swimming for what seemed like forever, going outward and not up. And then the tossing of waves suddenly stopped, and the pull of the ocean disappeared. Locking hands, they swam upward, breaking the surface and both greedily gasping for air.

He cried out, reaching for her as she did the same. Their lips touched, then fused together as one.

"Broch!" Brodee called. Broch broke the kiss with his wife and pulled back to answer his brother. "Aye! I have her. Gavin?"

"Dead," Brodee called back.

Broch could just see Katreine's silhouette in the moonlight. "How the devil will we make the rocks?"

"Follow me, Husband," she said proudly. "I'll guide ye."

"I'd follow ye anywhere," he assured her.

"Verra smart, ye are," she said, kissing him again. "'Tis

why ye are a legend."

"Nay, I was driven by a need, which made me a legend. Now the need is gone, and I'm content. From this day forward, I just want to be Broch Blackswell—husband, son, father."

"Father? Well then, we need to make haste to land so we can make those bairns."

He tugged her to him and kissed her warm lips. "Lead the way, Hellion. Lead the way."

Epilogue

Katreine sat at the dais in the Blackswell great hall with Broch by her side. As she pushed at the food on her trencher, he set a hand on her arm. A concerned look came to his face. "Are ye feeling unwell?"

"Aye," she grumbled. "The bairn dunnae ever stop kicking!"

He smiled at her. "She's going to be just like ye—a hellion."

"I'm a gentle lass now," Katreine insisted in a stern tone.

Broch chuckled at that. "Aye, ye are, and I'm but yer simple husband."

She knew he was teasing her, but her worry that he might need more than to live such a calm life niggled at her. She rubbed a finger over the place where he had once worn the ring that signified him as the King's right hand. Brodee wore the ring now, and he'd left a sennight ago on orders from the king to hunt down William, who had still not returned from his journey to the Dark Riders.

"I fear ye will miss it," she whispered. "The things that go with making ye a legend."

Broch leaned toward her and grazed his lips across her shoulder, making the babe kick and her shiver. "Nae ever, Wife. I am content and complete. All I ever need is here." He kissed her lips as his hand settled on her belly. "My family."

She placed her hand over his as her heart filled with joy. "Our family," she said, leaning into her husband, her rock, her legend.

Thank you so much for reading Broch and Katreine's story! I hope you enjoyed it! It would mean a great deal to me if you would consider leaving a review. Your opinion helps other readers find me, and it helps them decide whether to purchase my book or not. If you'd like to share your thoughts about the book, you can follow this link: *When a Highlander Weds a Hellion, Book 8.*
juliejohnstoneauthor.com/when-a-highlander-weds-a-hellion-8

If you loved my **HIGHLANDER VOWS: ENTANGLED HEARTS** series then I think you will love my new Historical Romance series, **RENEGADE SCOTS**! The first book in the series, **OUTLAW KING**, is now available. You can read the blurb and the prologue below and purchase it by going HERE. juliejohnstoneauthor.com/outlaw-king

She's the weapon intended to destroy him. He's the key to her freedom.

Dark days have come to Scotland, and fierce warrior Robert the Bruce would do anything to release his country from English rule—and not just because he's the rightful heir to the Scottish throne. As the bloody war rages on, enemies on both sides of the fight surround him, and Robert must dance a dangerous line between truth and deception. One misstep could topple his nation and cost him his life, yet one woman tempts him—and threatens his mission—as no other ever has.

Elizabeth de Burgh longs for freedom in a time when women have none. So when she finds herself ordered by her ruthless father and her godfather, the King of England, to seduce the leader of the Scottish rebellion and reveal his secrets, she yearns to fight back against their cruel plot. But they threaten to kill her beloved cousin, leaving her no choice but to comply. As she grows close to Robert and the mask that hides the man who would be king is peeled away, she cannot imagine aiding in the destruction of the noble Scot bent on liberating his people.

Bound by duty and honor but ensnared by passion, Robert and Elizabeth must determine if they are each other's biggest threat or greatest source of strength. And moreover, they must decide how much they are willing to risk for the one thing neither ever imagined they'd find with the other—extraordinary, boundless love.

Prologue

1296
Northern Scotland

Revolt had its own scent. It was one of burning wood and flesh, fetid wounds and rancid sweat, and it lay heavy in the air. Robert the Bruce, Earl of Carrick, smelled it with every breath he took.

"Rebellion surrounds us," Laird Niall Campbell said, pride ringing in his voice.

Bright-orange flames leaped into the sky from the destroyed guard towers that flanked the raised drawbridge to Andrew Moray's castle, which Robert had been commanded to invade. *Commanded.* The word reverberated in his head, making his temples throb. He glanced to his friend who sat mounted beside him. Perspiration trickled down Robert's back beneath his battle armor, and the moans of captured men reached his ears. Gut-hollowing guilt choked him. "We're on the wrong side of the fight," he said low, acknowledging out loud what they both knew.

Niall hitched a bushy red eyebrow as hope alighted in his eyes. "Dunnae tease me, Robbie," he whispered, ever careful, though they were far enough away from Richard Og de Burgh that the King of England's man would not be able to hear them. "Dunnae say such a thing unless ye are ready to disregard yer father's dictate."

"I'm ready," Robert replied, meaning it. The desire to follow his heart and defy his father, who demanded blind obedience to a plan that no longer had worth, had been building for months. Now, in this moment, it felt as if it would cleave him in two, it beat so strongly within him.

The time was not yet ripe to act, his father kept claiming. It was, and it had to be, now. Today. He could not take up arms against his own countrymen. He could no longer submit to his father's foolish order to remain aligned with King Edward in hope of gaining the Scottish throne, which had been stolen from their family by the usurper John Balliol.

"I'm a Scot, for Christ's sake," he muttered.

"Have nae I been reminding ye of that verra fact for nigh a year?" Niall's hand lay on the hilt of his sword revealing the danger of what they were about to do.

"Ye have, my friend, ye have," Robert said, his mind swiftly turning. His father should now rightfully be King of Scots, but instead Robert sat here ordered by the ever reaching King of England to destroy a stronghold in the land he loved, while his father seemed perfectly content to stay in England amid the comfort of the Bruces' plush English holdings rather than venture back to the wilds of Scotland to rise against King Edward and risk losing everything. Robert could no longer deny the truth—his father lacked the iron will to do what was right.

War meant blood, strife, and possibly death, but subjugation to an English king was a different sort of death, one of the spirit. He could not live that way. "We'll no longer be safe if we rise against Edward this day," he said, accepting it, but wanting to give Niall, who was married and had a daughter, one last chance to change his mind and keep his submission to Edward intact.

Niall snorted. "I thrive on danger."

God knew that was true enough. Niall had always been right there with Robert at the front of every battle, even on the day the Scot's daughter had been born. Still…

"We will be hunted," Robert added.

"Let them try to catch us," Niall said with a smirk. "The devil English king will nae stop until he sits on the throne of Scotland. He will kill all who continue to rebel, and that includes our people. I'd rather be hunted than aligned with King Edward."

"We will be outlaws, enemies of Edward."

"Shut up, Robbie," Niall growled using the nickname only those close to him dared use. "Quit trying to dissuade me. Ye need me."

"I do, but yer wife and yer daughter—"

"My wife will dance a jig when she hears we've taken up arms with our countrymen. Dunnae fash yerself. Tell me what ye want me to do."

Robert slid his teeth back and forth, contemplating that very question. He needed to be canny and proceed in the best way to protect his men. The wind blew from the west, sending billows of white smoke and heat toward them and de Burgh—the king's closest friend and advisor—who was mounted on his steed, some thirty paces ahead of them. De Burgh looked away, but Robert faced the wind. He, too, would suffer every hardship he demanded his men to endure, and most of the men who had ridden here on his command were in the path of the smoke. It burned his throat, nose, and eyes, making breathing nearly impossible.

Death by fire would be an awful way to die.

Robert swiped a gloved hand across his watering eyes and focused on the falconry building that stood vulnerable behind them. It was on the wrong side of the moat—the land unprotected by the drawbridge. Counting, his gaze moved over the captured Scots lined up in front of the outbuilding by de Burgh's men. Twenty of the Scot rebel Andrew Moray's men would die this day on de Burgh's command, unless the Moray warriors lowered their drawbridge and sent their lord, a leader of the Scottish uprising against Edward, out. Robert could not allow their deaths or Moray's.

"Andrew Moray!" De Burgh bellowed toward the castle, which was separated from them by the moat alone. The powerful Irish noble's accent sounded especially thick with anger. "Lower your drawbridge and surrender, or we'll burn your men alive."

Robert's hands tightened reflexively on his reins as the captured men moaned their protest, only to be silenced by the swords upon their chests, no doubt pricking flesh in warning. There was no more time to ponder. He had to act. These men would not lower the drawbridge.

De Burgh was a fool to think he could ride here from England and command these Scots. They hated Edward for his attempt to put himself on a throne he had no right to occupy. "Ride to the head of my men," he said to Niall, "and wait for my signal. If I can avoid bloodshed I will."

"Och," Niall said, "blood will be shed this day, but it will nae be Scot's blood."

"We can nae guarantee that, Niall," Robert replied.

Niall nodded. "I ken," he said, his shoulders sagging a bit. "Try to prevent a battle then," he relented, "but I feel in my bones it's imminent."

Robert felt it too, but he had a responsibility to do all he could to protect his vassals. "Go to the men," he urged.

With a nod, Niall turned his horse from Robert and headed down the hill toward Robert's vassals. Three hundred and fifty of his men who were loyal to him stood mixed with three hundred and fifty of the king's men. Robert clicked his heels against his steed's side and closed the distance between himself and de Burgh who flicked his gaze at Robert and then yelled toward the castle, "You do not have long to decide!"

"De Burgh," Robert growled, "ye can nae burn alive innocent men. They follow Moray's orders."

De Burgh jerked his head toward Robert. "Innocent?" he snarled. "These Scots rebel against Edward, their liege lord. They deserve their fate."

"Edward is nae their liege lord," Robert said through clenched teeth. "John Balliol was their king." The words sliding from his tongue were bitter but true.

"They should be glad to see such a weak king as Balliol driven from the throne," de Burgh retorted.

"Edward's plan all along, I'm certain," Robert snapped.

De Burgh flashed a smile. "Your people are the ones who appointed Edward to choose the next king of Scotland, all those years ago, if you recall. And he saw Balliol as the man with the best claim to the throne."

"He saw Balliol's weakness, and my grandfather's strength, and that's why Edward chose Balliol," Robert growled.

"You sound as if you wish to rebel," de Burgh said, smirking. "Where is your father, then?" De Burgh made a show of twisting around in his horse as if searching for Robert's father before facing Robert once more. His lip curled back in a taunting smile. "Ah yes, your father does not have the fortitude to rule Scotland. If he did, he would have risen in rebellion with the people who would fight against Edward in Balliol's name. Fall in line with me, Bruce," de Burgh threatened. "You have no other choice."

"There's always a choice," he spit out, finding the hilt of his sword and flicking his gaze toward Niall and Robert's vassals some one hundred yards behind them. Robert looked to de Burgh once more and motioned toward the captured men. "Release them."

"You insolent, foolish pup!" de Burgh growled, spittle flying from his mouth. "Stand down! Moray!" de Burgh roared. "I give you to the count of ten before I order my guards to fill the outbuilding with your men, and we can all watch them burn."

A window at the front of the castle banged open, and a woman—Lady Moray, Robert realized—appeared. "My husband is nae here, so we kinnae send him out."

De Burgh snorted. "She expects us to believe Moray did not come here to gather more men?"

"Perhaps he did nae," Robert said, seeing a chance to prevent bloodshed. "Moray rebels by the renegade William Wallace's side, and Wallace's men keep to the woods. Perhaps Moray went there first."

"I don't believe it," de Burgh snapped. To Lady Moray he shouted, "Lower your bridge. I will see for myself if you speak the truth."

"Nay, ye Irish scum! Ye simper and cater to the English king!" Lady Moray bellowed.

Robert's fingers curled tighter around the cool iron of his sword. There would be war today, after all. Lady Moray had just shot an arrow of barbed words at a man who wore his pride like a cloak.

De Burgh's face turned purple. "Burn them!" he cried, his voice trembling with rage. The two guards standing near the door rushed to open it, and as they did, de Burgh flicked his hand to a slight guard who held the torch. "Set the fire when the door is closed."

Shouts erupted from the captured warriors, and Robert's blood rushed through his veins and roared in his ears. His life was about to change forever. But his honor would remain intact. He would rise in rebellion, not for Balliol to be returned to the throne as king, but for the people of Scotland to keep their freedom. He could worry of nothing else now.

The terrified shouts of Moray's men as they were locked in the falconry pierced the roar of blood in his ears. "Tell yer men to halt," Robert yelled to de Burgh. "Do so now and take yer leave from Moray's land, or I'll kill ye." His heart beat like a drum.

De Burgh bared his teeth. "You have misplaced your loyalty, Bruce."

Robert flicked his gaze past de Burgh, over the rocky ground that separated the two of them from the warriors in the distance, to Niall at the front of Robert's vassals. He raised his right hand and swiveled it round, giving the signal to rebel.

Niall smiled, a flash of white against his sun-bronzed skin. He raised his own hand and returned the signal. They would live or die this day, but they would do it with honor.

Tension vibrated through every part of Robert's body as he yelled, "To arms for Scotland!"

All at once, the hissing, scraping, sliding, and singing of seven hundred blades filled the air, and the clashing of steel sounded in the distance. A woman's scream ripped through the noise, shocking Robert by how close it was. De Burgh swung his sword at Robert, but Robert parlayed the blow and unseated de Burgh with one move. With no time to waste, he turned his horse toward the outbuilding, and he gaped at the scene before him. The squire who held the torch was running from de Burgh's guards and toward

Robert. The young man suddenly swerved toward the moat and threw the torch toward it. The bright flame disappeared into the water, and Robert raced to save the man who would likely be killed for his actions.

Robert met the guards halfway to the squire, who was now running back toward him. He parried a blow from the left, then the right, and caught a glimpse of Niall riding fast toward him.

"Release the trapped men!" he yelled to the Campbell, but in a breath, de Burgh's warriors descended on his friend, now engaged in a battle for his life.

Behind Robert, the loud grating of the drawbridge being lowered stilled all motion for a moment. God's teeth! Surely, Lady Moray was not lowering it in surrender. Within a breath, the thundering of hundreds of horses' hooves against the wooden bridge set a buzz in the air that seemed to vibrate into Robert's very bones.

When he glanced around for the squire, he saw nothing but English knights heading toward him. He raised his sword in defense of an oncoming hit, knocked the blade out of the knight's hand, and nudged his mount out of the way of another Englishman. It had turned him directly toward the bridge where Lady Moray herself came riding out, her red hair billowing behind her as she led her husband's warriors in a charge. They appeared to number almost two hundred, not near enough that they could have withstood an attack from the combined forces of the Bruce men and the English garrison, but they had more than enough to overcome the English if the lady intended to join forces with Robert. But did she?

As she rode, she shouted, "Free our men. Free our men! Someone free our men!"

Robert swept his gaze back to the outbuilding, and the

breath was snatched from his chest. The young squire had somehow managed to get to the outbuilding. Niall was there, as well, along with six more of Robert's men. They held the English guards back, but one broke free and raised his sword to strike down the squire as he stepped toward the door and seemed to be opening it. Robert ripped his dagger from its sheath and flung it with all his might toward the knight. The dagger pierced the man's hand as he was bringing his sword down and he dropped his weapon. The squire, who'd turned toward his attacker, eyes wide with fear, twisted back around to the door and slung it open. Moray's men poured out, weaponless.

Robert unhooked his shield from his saddle, and then dismounted amid the chaos, his sword in one hand and his shield in the other. He raced toward the stumbling Moray men and the squire, parrying blows as he went. When he reached the boy, a call to fire at the lad and the Moray men went out from de Burgh. Cursing, Robert looked to his right to find that a line of knights had covered the distance from the scrimmage below to the castle, and they were lined up to shoot. Robert shoved the boy behind him, as a volley of arrows flew through the air. They clanked against his shield.

"Again!" de Burgh shouted, clearly not caring if he struck down his own men.

Robert moved to shield the boy once more, but the squire stepped out from behind Robert and ripped off his helmet. Long blond hair tumbled out over his—no, her—shoulders. Robert could do no more than stare in shock at de Burgh's daughter, Elizabeth de Burgh. Her clear blue gaze met his for a brief moment.

"Cease fire! Cease fire!" came de Burgh's frantic call.

The chit's eyes, bluer than any Robert had ever beheld,

widened with what appeared to be shock. Had she thought her father may not save her?

She turned to Robert. "Thank you for your aid, my lord." The words tumbled from her mouth in a rush, and then to Robert's surprise, she dashed, as graceful as a deer fleeing a predator, past him and toward her father.

Robert stood dumbfounded for a moment at the young chit he'd seen at court but had never met. One of his men lunged toward her, and Robert shouted, "Leave her!"

She raced through the melee, surprisingly agile and quick, and she managed to reach her father unscathed. At once, she was snatched up by the hand she stretched toward her father and slung on the back of the destrier he had mounted once again.

Lady Moray and her husband's warriors came into the fray of the battle that was now moving ever closer. English arrows flew toward them. She raised a hand as she raced forward, and Robert looked to the rampart of the castle, relieved to see four dozen or so bowmen. Within a breath, more arrows soared through the air, but this time toward the knights lined up to shoot at her. As she reached Robert, he said, "My lady, I would stand in defense of yer home if ye will allow me to."

She arched her eyebrows over glittering gray eyes. "It's about time a Bruce came to his senses," she said with a nod. "I'll fight alongside ye, for this day ye have saved many Moray lives."

Robert glanced around at the already fallen men from both sides and made a decision. "De Burgh!" he bellowed, before any more casualties came to pass. "The Moray men fight with me. Stand down and leave, or be prepared to die."

De Burgh twisted his mount toward Robert while calling an order to his men to hold, and Robert did the same to his and Lady Moray's men. De Burgh was an astute man. He had to see he was outnumbered and that the best option would be to flee as Robert had graciously offered to allow.

"I name you traitor, Bruce, and I'll inform King Edward of your treachery."

"I can nae be a traitor to a man I do nae call king!" Robert reminded de Burgh. A roar of approval arose from his men and the Moray men alike.

A command to his men to depart was the answer from de Burgh, and the English garrison quickly complied, taking their mounts and turning to ride out. As Robert watched them leave, Elizabeth de Burgh twisted in the saddle, her unwavering gaze meeting his.

Beside him, Lady Moray spoke. "That girl forever has my debt. I pray the punishment for her deeds this day are not too grave.

Robert nodded. Elizabeth de Burgh had mettle, that much was certain. It would remain to be seen if it was not beaten out of her after today.

"What will ye do now?" Lady Moray asked.

Robert thought briefly of his father ensconced in Durham at one of their English manors. He would need to send a messenger to give his father fair warning of what had occurred this day. What he did with that information was on his head.

"My lord?" Lady Moray said.

He caught the lady's inquisitive gaze. "I'll send word to my father of my actions—"

"*Honorable actions*," she said, reaching out and squeezing his forearm.

He inclined his head in gratitude, certain his father would not feel the same. Swallowing a sudden swell of emotion for the rift he had placed between himself and his father this day, he said, "then I'll ride to Hugh Eglinton's Castle. I've received word that the nobility leading the rebellion have been given safe haven there to meet and plan, and amongst the party is also William Wallace."

Lady Moray's eyebrows arched. She bit her lip for a moment then spoke. "Ye ken many of those men fight in the name of Balliol. They fight for his return to the throne."

"Aye," Robert replied. "But Balliol abdicated and I have heard that the Comyns—" saying the name of his family's bitter enemies who years before had put the force of their great power behind their cousin Balliol to have him named as the man with the best claim to the throne over Robert's grandfather, always made Robert's throat tighten. "—are imprisoned by Edward. I go to fight for Scotland, as I did this day."

She nodded. "I pray for ye that it will be enough to see ye well."

"I'll gladly take yer prayers, he replied, sensing deep within that he would need them.

"I'll send a messenger ahead of ye with word of yer deeds for me to my husband who is at Eglinton Castle," she revealed with a secretive smile. "That way, ye are more likely to keep yer head when ye approach the Scots. Many think ye a traitor."

"I know it well," Robert said, "but I will face it and prove them wrong. Do nae risk yer man."

"I owe ye," she whispered fiercely. "Ye saved my men. I will pay my debt by aiding ye in hopefully saving yer life when ye approach Eglinton. Grant!" Lady Moray bellowed and within a breath a young Scottish warrior appeared. Lady Moray smiled at the young man mounted beside her. "Grant rides like the wind. He should reach the castle before yer large gathering of vassals." Robert inclined his head at her words. To Grant, she said, "Ride to yer laird. Take word of Bruce's actions here today, and tell my husband, Bruce is our friend."

"I will, my lady," the warrior said, before turning his horse and galloping away. They watched him in silence for a moment before Lady Moray spoke again. "Dunnae tarry, Bruce. Scotland needs yer fighting strength. Ride hard."

"I vow it!" he swore, turned from Lady Moray, and gave the signal for his men to follow suit. Niall brought his horse beside Robert's and together they led the men away from Moray's castle. As they did, Robert felt Niall's steady gaze upon him. "What is it?" Robert finally asked.

"Please tell me this means we dunnae ever have to go back to the English court and pretend to admire the English king nor like English food."

Robert chuckled, some of the tension unknotting from his shoulders. "God willing. Niall, I will ride to Eglinton with my men to join the rebellion are ye certain ye wish to ride with me? What of yer clan, yer wife, yer daughter?"

"My clan is secure under my brother's care in my absence. As for my wife and daughter, it is thanks to ye that my daughter is alive. Dunnae think I've ever forgotten, nor has Calissa, how ye saved our Brianna when those English knights captured her. Brianna is safe at home with Calissa, and I will stay with ye and fight for our land and to free our people."

"If ye ride with me, ye may ride to yer death," Robert said, his tone grave.

"I've ridden next to ye since we were young and trained together at the Earl of Mar's castle, Robbie. If I'm to ride to my death, there is nae anyone I'd rather be beside, but I think we ride to freedom. Let us see it together, aye?"

"Aye," Robert agreed. There would be no changing Niall's mind, and Robert both appreciated his friend's loyalty and feared for him. But Niall's decision was set, and there were no arguments left to be made, so Robert urged his steed into a gallop to which his men matched the pace.

They rode relentlessly through the remains of the day, over hard terrain, under the baking sun, and into the early evening hours. When he finally spotted Eglinton Castle in the distance, he ordered the party to halt and turned to Niall. "I'll venture up alone," he announced, determined to protect Niall should the other Scottish nobility greet them with swords and wish to fight, despite Lady Moray's sending word. Many saw them as traitors, thanks to his father's orders to continue obeying Edward even when the Scottish nobility started to rebel against his rule, and Robert was not convinced Lady Moray's words would have much effect on those who distrusted him.

"The devil ye will," Niall replied, his tone hard. "I'm nae going to linger back here with the men and let ye get all the glory. I'll go with ye, thank ye. All those who dared to call us traitors will ken the part I played in striking against de Burgh and, therefore, the English king."

Robert opened his mouth to argue and then promptly shut it. It would do no good. "Ye're as stubborn as a goat," he grumbled instead. "And I do nae have time to mince words with ye. Come along."

Niall chuckled as they moved their horses down the path that wound up to the castle gates. As they rode, Niall said, "It's heartening to see that ye have finally learned I'm the stronger of the two of us."

"If ye think I'd ever believe that," Robert teased, "ye must have hit yer head."

"Name yerself," a guard bellowed, interrupting their

banter as they approached the gate.

"Robert the Bruce."

"Laird Niall Campbell," Niall added.

"The turncoat arrives," the guard hissed.

It was as Robert had expected. He whipped his sword up to the man's throat. "I'm nae a turncoat. My family did nae support Balliol, but that does nae mean I will nae fight for Scotland against Edward."

"Come along, then," the guard relented in a begrudging tone. "The others will decide if ye should keep yer head."

"Everyone always wants my head," Robert said lightheartedly, "yet it still sits upon my shoulders."

Niall chuckled, and the guard glared at the two of them. He guided them up the stone steps, past more guards, and into the torchlit castle. Silence blanketed much of the estate at such a late hour, but muffled voices drifted from down a dark corridor. A flicker of light flamed at the end. The guard stopped and motioned toward it. "The leaders of the rebellion are in the great hall discussing strategy."

Robert nodded, and he and Niall fell into step behind the guard once more. As they made their way down the corridor, the voices coming from the great hall grew louder and more distinct.

"I'm nae going to risk my life to put Bruce on the throne!" someone bellowed.

Robert flinched, knowing they were referring to his father.

The guard who was with them snickered, and Robert glared the man into silence.

"Bruce is the rightful claimant," came another voice.

"Bah! Bruce swore fealty to Edward as overlord of Scotland!"

"Ye ken he did that to avoid swearing allegiance to

Balliol!" someone else shouted.

"Where is he, then?" the other man thundered. "Balliol has abdicated, and Bruce, the elder, does nae return to Scotland to help us stop Edward. What does he do instead? He sits in his lavish English estate! He has no backbone to rebel! Let us look to John Comyn to lead us in Balliol's absence. He has managed to escape the imprisonment that befell many in his family."

Their words were like harsh blows to Robert's chest. John "the Red" Comyn came from one of the most powerful families in Scotland—Robert's being the other—and that was the heart of the conflict between his family and the Comyns. The Comyns wanted all the power, including the throne, but not for the good of Scotland—for greed. Comyn cared for the rebellion only insomuch as he wished to protect his vast estates and current power. He did not truly care for the people and their freedom.

Robert gritted his teeth. He would have to fight beside a man who wanted to destroy him in order to save the land he loved. He shoved the guard out of the way, but a hand came to his arm. He turned to find Niall staring at him. "I'll nae bend the knee to a Comyn," Niall said. "Ye ken as well as I do that they will do all they can to gain the throne if there is nae any hope to return Balliol to it."

Robert nodded. "We will fight for Scotland." He didn't say that he hoped his father would join them, though the hope lingered.

Suddenly, the door was flung open, and a giant of a man appeared at the threshold. He had to duck to exit the great hall. He strode toward Robert and Niall, his boots thudding against the floor. He stopped in front of them and smiled, a genuine expression that reached his clear blue eyes and made them crinkle at the edges. "I thought I heard a noise out here," he said in a deep, friendly voice.

"Ye heard us despite all the commotion within?" Robert asked, exchanging a quick glance with Niall.

"Aye." The Scot nodded as he scratched at his russet beard. "I've had to learn to listen carefully, especially when surrounded by chaos. 'Tis how I still survive though the English hunt me. I'm William Wallace of Elderslie."

"We've heard of ye," Niall replied. "I'm sorry to hear about yer wife."

Grief swept over Wallace's face for the space of a breath before murderous rage replaced it. "I thank ye. The English are suffering for the murder of my wife and will continue to do so. And ye are?" His curious gaze took in both Robert and Niall.

"Niall Campbell."

"Carrick," Robert said, giving only his title, as was customary.

"Ah, Bruce," Wallace said, ignoring the given title. "Word of yer deeds have been brought to us by a messenger from Lady Moray."

Robert nodded Wallace grinned. "Seems ye made a friend in the lady and she thought to save yer head should anyone want to take it off." He gazed intently at Robert. "Why have ye come here to us?"

"To help retain Scotland's freedom, just as ye, Wallace." Wallace looked unconvinced, so Robert added, "I've heard some things about ye as well."

"Aye? What do they say?" he asked, a twinkle in his eyes.

"That ye fight like a brute beast."

Wallace chuckled. "How would ye have me fight?"

"To win," Robert replied easily enough.

Wallace set a large hand on Robert's shoulder. "I do

believe ye are the first noble I've met that I have actually liked," Wallace said, winking at Robert. "Let us see if my opinion is enough to keep yer head on yer shoulders."

Robert nodded and fell into step with Niall by his side behind Wallace. Wallace entered the room of disagreeing Scottish nobles and rebels, and when Robert and Niall followed all arguing ceased, chairs scraped, and the singing of swords being unsheathed filled the air.

England

Elizabeth pressed her hands against the cold glass of her bedchamber window, which overlooked the beautiful gardens at the king's court. Her breath caught when her father and the king turned to look up at her as one. She scurried back from the window and bumped into the table behind her. The vase teetered, and she lunged for it, catching it before it hit the floor. But her foot slid out in front of her, and she went down with a hard *thud*, the breath whooshing out of her and the water in the vase spilling down the front of her gown.

She sat there with her bottom pulsing in pain, and her mind awhirl with horrid possibilities about what punishment the king was demanding her father dole out after what she'd done at the Moray's castle. Banishment from her parents, her brothers, and sisters to some remote place? A nunnery for life? She shuddered. She may only be twelve summers, as her mother and older sister always loved to remind her, but she did know some things, contrary to what they seemed to believe. She understood fully that she had far too much zest for life to spend hers in a nunnery or someday be a docile wife, for that matter. She inhaled a long breath and tried to slow her racing heart. Her father loved her. He would reason with the king. He would protect her.

Wouldn't he?

Worry niggled at her as she set down the vase beside her and drew her legs to her chest, shivering with a chill of which she could not seem to rid herself. The memory of her father giving the order to burn men alive filled her mind. There had to be some explanation. There simply had to be. Because if there was not, then her father was not the man she believed him to be. And if he was not good and honorable, then how could she trust he'd protect her?

Still quivering, she set her palms to the cold, wet floor and scooted over enough to see in the slash of sunlight coming through the window. She could recall her father's face just before he had locked her in this bedchamber, and the hairs on the back of her neck prickled. Never had she seen such rage from him. He'd been nearly purple and unable to speak, and it said a great deal that he had not come to see her even once in the past sennight, nor had he allowed her out of her bedchamber. She had thought he would have by now. In fact, she had been sure he would visit so he could tell her he was vexed, very vexed, but that he loved her and had been compelled somehow to give the horrific order to burn the men.

She twined her hair around her finger, her agitation increasing. She was not sure how much longer she could endure being locked in here alone. The only person she had seen since returning home was the chambermaid who brought Elizabeth a tray of food three times a day and emptied her pot. She let out a ragged sigh. Perhaps she should be grateful she was being fed. She began to rock back and forth, going through the events which had led her to disguise herself as a squire and ride out with her father, his men, and Lord Carrick, Robert the Bruce.

It had been two things truly. She'd been irritated that her father had dismissed her request to ride with him that day so completely, loudly, and publicly. She'd not known the "mission," but she had known she wanted to be part of it, and she could not see why she should not. Father had always allowed her to do things other girls did not. She rode as a man did, she spoke her mind, and she had even accompanied her father and his men on hunts.

The other compelling factor had been Lord Carrick himself. She had not met him, though the young man had been at court for some time. He was always surrounded by other lords and lavishly dressed women batting their eyelashes at him, but it was the way his dark gaze looked through the ladies and the simpering lords as if they were not there—or perhaps as if he wished to be anywhere but there himself—that intrigued her so. Once she had overheard her father tell the king that Bruce concerned him. He feared the young lord harbored secret compassion for the wretched Scots' cause. Those words had burrowed into her heart, for she secretly thought that it was wrong of her godfather to try to make himself king of a land to which he had not been born, to a people who did not want him as their king. She did not dare utter such a thing out loud, of course; even she knew it was foolish to *always* speak one's mind.

A soft tap came at the door followed by, "Elizabeth?" in a low, worried murmur.

Elizabeth jumped to her feet at her cousin's voice, nearly slipping in her haste. "Lillianna!" she cried out, pressing her palms to the thick, dark wood of the door. Never had she been so happy to hear her dearest friend's voice.

Lillianna was more of a sister to Elizabeth than her three true sisters were. Lillianna was the only female Elizabeth knew who shared her leanings toward things that were considered restricted to women—riding as a man, archery, swimming, and learning more than how to select food for supper and embroidery. Her cousin also was an excellent eavesdropper, a talent she'd taught Elizabeth when Lillianna had come to live with them two years ago after the death of her mother.

"I'm so glad to hear your voice!" Elizabeth said. "What news do you bring? Is it terrible? Am I to be banished? What did you learn?"

"Not very much, I'm afraid," Lillianna moaned. "Whatever has been decided about your fate has thus far been discussed behind doors too thick for eavesdropping. I'm not even supposed to be here. Your mother and father expressly forbade me from coming to see you, and Aveline has been trailing me, keeping watch."

Elizabeth rolled her eyes at her sister older Aveline being her usual perfectly awful self. "How did you manage to escape her?"

Lillianna snickered. "I told her Guy de Beauchamp wished to see her in the solar."

"Oh, Lillianna!" Elizabeth laughed, feeling so grateful for her cousin and only true friend. "Aveline will be livid when she learns you tricked her. She has a tendre for Lord de Beauchamp. Though I cannot see why. There is something about him that unsettles me."

"Perhaps it's the way he is always staring at you as if you are a great treasure he wishes to add to his collection when you become of age," Lillianna said sarcastically.

"I will never marry a man such as Guy de Beauchamp," Elizabeth vowed. "I don't care if he is one of the wealthiest lords in the land. Aveline can have him!"

"As if you will have a choice of who you marry." Sadness blanketed Lillianna's voice.

Elizabeth wished she could hug her cousin. Lillianna was likely thinking of her mother, who'd been forced to marry her father. Uncle Brice had beaten Lillianna's mother for being unfaithful, and she had died from the beating. But being a powerful lord, he had gone unpunished for the death of a simple Scottish lass.

Elizabeth inhaled deeply, refusing to worry about problems that were years off. "We shall both use our very clever minds to come up with a plot to marry men of our own choosing. We will aid each other!"

"You are so naive and hopeful, Elizabeth. 'Tis one of the reasons I adore you so. I cannot linger, though I wish I could. I came to warn you that your mother is coming to see you today."

Elizabeth tensed. Her mother never had a kind word for her, only criticism, and Elizabeth could only imagine what she would say about ignoring her father's orders. Likely, she was livid. Not out of care for Elizabeth, of course, but out of fury over being embarrassed at court by Elizabeth's actions. "You better depart, then. I'd not want Mother to take out her vexation with me on you." And her mother would; Lillianna knew this. Mother cared for Lillianna even less than she did Elizabeth, which was barely at all. Elizabeth felt sure her cousin had only been permitted to come live with them because it had made Mother look charitable and warm-hearted.

"I'll return tonight if I'm able," Lillianna said.

"Only if it's safe. I don't want you bringing trouble to yourself on my account."

"I'll be careful," Lillianna promised, then the tap of her footsteps fell on the floor.

Elizabeth stood there listening until the sound of Lillianna's departure faded. Silence descended momentarily but was broken once more by the tap of shoes upon the floor. She sucked in a sharp breath, fearing it was her mother. She hoped Lillianna had not been seen.

A distinct jangling of keys and the clink of a lock made Elizabeth's heart race. The door opened, and her mother, looking perfectly coifed and richly garbed, stepped into the room. Blue eyes that she'd been told a thousand times were the same color as hers narrowed on Elizabeth. "You cannot depart this room looking like that."

Her mother's unfriendly tone made her clench her teeth, but the news that she was to depart hit her like a ray of hope. "I'm to be released? I'm forgiven?"

"Forgiven?" Sarcasm laced Mother's words. She stepped in front of Elizabeth, close enough that she got a full whiff of the pungent oil her mother liked to wear. "You are not forgiven. You are lucky to still have your head, you silly, willful girl!"

The slap came fast and hard, leaving a sting that brought tears to Elizabeth's eyes.

"Marietta!" Elizabeth's father boomed from the doorway. "Don't raise your hand to Elizabeth again!" Relief flowed through Elizabeth, but as her father settled his dark, unfriendly gaze on her, it vanished. "She has to be taken through the great hall to depart, and I'll not have anyone seeing her skin marred with red welts that will remind them of her deed."

"She is the talk of the court!" her mother wailed. "Let them see we punished her!"

Elizabeth's stomach knotted at her mother's words.

"Clearly, you have not been in the Great Hall this morning," her father said to her mother. "Elizabeth's deed is no longer on everyone's lips. Bruce is the talk of the court now," her father said, his voice lethal. "It seems he left the rebel Moray's castle and rode from there to join the other Scottish lords and renegades to rise against Edward."

"Pity," her mother murmured. "I had a hope to marry Aveline to Bruce but that won't do now. He'll lose his estates for certain."

Her father frowned. "I have a marriage in mind for Aveline already, so don't vex yourself. Now, wait outside. I wish to speak with Elizabeth alone."

"Richard," her mother exclaimed, "you promised me I would have charge of her now!"

The news made Elizabeth cringe.

"Woman!" her father roared. "You will, but you will have it *after* I have spoken to her."

Her mother, eyes wide and no doubt sensing she had pushed Father as far as he would be pushed, backed out of the room, shutting the door as she left.

Elizabeth pressed her back against the wall, wishing she could disappear into it.

Her father's eyes seemed to harden as he looked at her. "You have made a fool of me."

Elizabeth clenched her hands. "Father, no. I—"

"Silence!" The word whipped across the space and hit her just as hard as her mother had.

She flinched away from him and fisted the slick material of her gown in her hands.

Her father's gaze raked over her. "I always had a particular tendre for you, so I allowed indulgencies I did not with your brothers and sisters, ones I should not have allowed."

Color rose in his cheeks as he spoke, and Elizabeth stared at the rosy bloom that spread down his neck. Father saying that he'd *had* a particular tendre for her echoed in her mind. Had she destroyed his love for her, then? Her belly felt suddenly hollow.

He swiped a hand across his red beard, tugging at the ends. "Your mother warned me that I was ruining you, making you into the opposite of what a lady should be—willful, too curious, wild—but I told her to mind her place." He shook his head. "I let you linger when I should have sent you away, and because of my weakness, you believe you can do as you please!" He banged a fist into his open palm. "You—" He pointed a finger at her. "You seem to think you have a place at the table of men!" His hand gripped her chin so swiftly she gasped. "I tell you now, you do not. You are a girl and will grow to be a lady, obedient and lovely, and you will learn that your purpose is to serve my house as I command for the furthering of the family. Do you understand me?"

She fought against the tremor in her body. She understood. Her importance to him lay only with what wealth or connections she could bring to the family one day, just as Aveline had always claimed. Elizabeth had not believed it until now. What a fool she'd been! She had no freedom, only the rights her father gave to her. Did he feel no true affection for her? Was there no explanation for the order he had given that day? Her mind spun, making her stomach roil.

Her father squeezed her chin. "Do. You. Understand?"

She stared at the pulsing vein near his right eye. She knew she ought to respond immediately, yet such worry coursed through her, she could not make herself speak, even knowing her silence would have grave repercussions.

"Elizabeth," he hissed, his color rising again. "Your head is currently on your shoulders because I convinced the king that you could be useful to him eventually. Should I tell him otherwise?"

The king? Her father had convinced Edward that she would be useful to him? But how? Gooseflesh swept down her arms as her father's fingers curled even deeper into her skin. "No," she managed to choke out.

"Good." He released her chin, and she rocked back from him, desperately wanting to rub her aching skin. Instead, she forced herself to fold her hands together and prayed she appeared calm.

Silence stretched between them, and he watched her steadily before he smiled. "You are stubborn and prideful, and you don't know your place. But you will learn it. By God you will." He grabbed her suddenly by the arm, half dragged her across the room, flung open the door, and shoved her toward her mother. "Take her home to Ireland, and make her into a lady who will benefit this family."

The anger and hurt deep inside Elizabeth burst within her and overcame her fear. "You would have burned men alive to keep the king's esteem," she accused with a desperate hope that he would deny it.

"Yes," he replied, his wintery voice and open acceptance of the awful truth making her feel as if her legs would buckle. She placed a steadying hand on the wall as the floor beneath her seemed to sway. "Do you think I became this rich and powerful without currying favors?" he demanded.

"Favors?" She heard herself gasp, yet her voice seemed very far away. Her ears rang horribly. "It is not simply a favor to burn men alive."

"I cannot allow anyone to defy me. *Ever.* That is how I stay powerful. You'd do well not to forget it, Daughter."

She would not forget. As much as it pained her, she would hold close the memory that her father had traded his honor for the king's continued support and the wealth it would bring. Never would she marry a man who would do such a thing.

Series by Julie Johnstone

Scottish Medieval Romance Books:

Highlander Vows: Entangled Hearts Series
When a Laird Loves a Lady, Book 1
Wicked Highland Wishes, Book 2
Christmas in the Scot's Arms, Book 3
When a Highlander Loses His Heart, Book 4
How a Scot Surrenders to a Lady, Book 5
When a Warrior Woos a Lass, Book 6
When a Scot Gives His Heart, Book 7
When a Highlander Weds a Hellion, Book 8
Highlander Vows: Entangled Hearts Boxset, Books 1-4

Renegade Scots Series
Outlaw King, Book 1
Highland Defender, Book 2

Regency Romance Books:

A Whisper of Scandal Series
Bargaining with a Rake, Book 1
Conspiring with a Rogue, Book 2
Dancing with a Devil, Book 3
After Forever, Book 4
The Dangerous Duke of Dinnisfree, Book 5

A Once Upon A Rogue Series
My Fair Duchess, Book 1
My Seductive Innocent, Book 2
My Enchanting Hoyden, Book 3
My Daring Duchess, Book 4

Lords of Deception Series
What a Rogue Wants, Book 1

Danby Regency Christmas Novellas
The Redemption of a Dissolute Earl, Book 1
Season For Surrender, Book 2
It's in the Duke's Kiss, Book 3

Regency Anthologies
A Summons from the Duke of Danby (Regency Christmas Summons, Book 2)
Thwarting the Duke (When the Duke Comes to Town, Book 2)

Regency Romance Box Sets
A Whisper of Scandal Trilogy (Books 1-3)
Dukes, Duchesses & Dashing Noblemen (A Once Upon a Rogue Regency Novels, Books 1-3)

Paranormal Books:

The Siren Saga
Echoes in the Silence, Book 1

About the Author

As a little girl I loved to create fantasy worlds and then give all my friends roles to play. Of course, I was always the heroine! Books have always been an escape for me and brought me so much pleasure, but it didn't occur to me that I could possibly be a writer for a living until I was in a career that was not my passion. One day, I decided I wanted to craft stories like the ones I loved, and with a great leap of faith I quit my day job and decided to try to make my dream come true. I discovered my passion, and I have never looked back. I feel incredibly blessed and fortunate that I have been able to make a career out of sharing the stories that are in my head! I write Scottish Medieval Romance, Regency Romance, and I have even written a Paranormal Romance book. And because I have the best readers in the world, I have hit the USA Today bestseller list several times.

If you love me, I hope you do, you can follow me on Bookbub, and they will send you notices whenever I have a sale or a new release. You can follow me here:
bookbub.com/authors/julie-johnstone

You can also join my newsletter to get great prizes and inside scoops!
Join here: https://goo.gl/qnkXFF

I really want to hear from you! It makes my day!
Email me here:
juliejohnstoneauthor@gmail.com

I'm on Facebook a great deal chatting about books and life. If you want to follow me, you can do so here:
facebook.com/authorjuliejohnstone

Can't get enough of me? Well, good! Come see me here:
Twitter:
@juliejohnstone
Goodreads:
https://goo.gl/T57MTA

Made in the USA
Middletown, DE
22 March 2019